Before The
The Septem

by

Joe Nathan Paul

2025

ISBN - 9798280383173

Cover design by: John Sidebottom

LEGAL DISCLAIMER

This book is a work of fiction. All names, characters, organisations, locations, and events are either products of the author's imagination or are used in a purely fictitious manner. Any resemblance to actual persons, living or deceased, or real-world events, places, or entities is purely coincidental and not intended to portray real individuals or situations.

The depiction of MI6, the CIA, NASA, the Vatican, the Smithsonian Institution, or any other real-world government, intelligence, religious, scientific, or corporate organisations is entirely fictionalised for dramatic and narrative purposes. No inference should be made regarding these entities' real-world actions, policies, or affiliations.

The novel explores the themes of power, control, and secrecy, but it does not endorse or promote conspiracy theories, misinformation, or speculative narratives about real governments, institutions, or global events. Any references to historical events, technological advancements, geopolitical strategies, or scientific theories are used solely for entertainment and storytelling purposes and should not be interpreted as real-world facts.

Furthermore, any real historical figures, public figures, or well-known individuals referenced within this book are used in a fictionalised context. Their inclusion does not imply endorsement, involvement, or factual accuracy concerning the events of this novel.

The author and publisher assume no responsibility or liability for how any part of this book is interpreted, used, or applied outside of its intended fictional context. Readers are encouraged to approach all real-world topics with critical thinking and reliance on verified sources of information.

FROM VISIONES STELLARUM, FRAGMENT XIII:1–8

(Translated from the sealed folios of the Codex Septem
Warburg Institute, Recovered 1978)

*And I looked, and the stars broke rank from the heavens.
And the voice of the seventh spiral did call—not with
thunder, but with memory. And a gate was opened where
none had been, and the riders came forth once more,
veiled in the stillness of judgment.*

*And the first bore the sign of conquest, but his crown was
ash. The second held war in his hand, and his blade
dripped ancient blood. The third carried a balance, but his
scales were broken. And the fourth—his name was not
Death, for Death remembers, and this one did not.*

*They came not from Heaven, nor from Earth, but from the
place beneath remembrance, where the old fires sleep.
And their breath was silence, and their eyes carried the
weight of reckoning.*

*And the world did not know them, though it had named
them long ago. For these were not omens, nor
punishments, but the return of that which once unmade the
stars. And the pattern began again.*

PROLOGUE

David Ross's office always looked like a war room on the brink of surrender — maps strewn like casualties, coffee mugs half-drained, notes scrawled across dog-eared pages. The walls hummed with tension. So did he.

Ross sat motionless, staring at a blurred photograph — an improvised jungle airstrip, crates stacked high, and something faintly wrong in the dirt. A mark? A shadow pretending not to be? A shape that didn't belong, one he'd seen before. He'd followed whispers across three continents, piecing together fragments no one else had the patience — or the paranoia — to see.

They called them ghosts. Coincidences. He knew better. Patterns. Rhythms. Echoes. And this time, they scared him because it wasn't just whispers. Not just loose ends or half-buried cables.

He'd stumbled on a black-budget operation that didn't officially exist — one that operated beneath oversight, behind military funding, and far beyond political reach. A machine with no name. No limits. And no leash.

1

In Bogota, a safe house had gone dark. Twenty-three dead. No entry logs. No exit wounds. Only that symbol, burnt into the wall.

He used to believe in coincidence. Now he believed in orchestration.

A knock broke his focus. He covered the photo without thinking.

'Come in. '

'You're popular today,' she said.

Carla Grant. Off-book liaison. Sharp-eyed, underpaid, and too principled for the building she worked in. She stepped in with a smirk that didn't reach her eyes.

Ross didn't smile. 'Not the kind of popular I'd recommend.'

She closed the door softly. 'So, who are you calling this time? More ghosts? Another clean team?'

Ross exhaled through his nose. 'People who don't rattle easily. '

'SAS?'

He gave the slightest nod.

'Why them?' she asked. 'Why not CIA? Or JSOC? You've got strings everywhere. '

Ross leaned back, tension shifting from his shoulders to his voice.

'Because I don't want bureaucracy. I don't want hesitation. I need men who know what the world looks like when the rules break down — and who'll still keep going. '

He met her eyes.

'The CIA will ask for jurisdiction. JSOC will want drone feeds and a dozen lawyers. But these guys? They'll go in quiet. Get the job done clean. And if it turns out I'm wrong...'

He tapped the photo.

'Then I'll take the blame. '

Carla tilted her head. 'What exactly are they walking into?'

Ross slid the photo across the desk. 'This. '

She squinted. 'Looks like cartel logistics. Crates, fuel drums, cheap airstrip. Nothing you haven't seen before. '

'Look again. '

She leaned in — and froze. Etched faintly onto the crate was a stylised horse. Rearing. Weather-worn, half-erased, but still watching.

Her voice dropped. 'You think it's them?'

Ross nodded. 'Every time we get close, something shifts. The data. The witnesses. The chain of evidence. It's like someone got there first. '

He paused.

'They leave things behind. Symbols. Corpses. Gaps. Like history got rewritten when we weren't looking. '

She stared at the photo, the lines on her face deepening. 'You think the SAS can handle this?'

Ross took the image back. His fingers tightened, knuckles whitening slightly.

'They have to. There's no one else I'd trust with this. '

Carla nodded, but the doubt lingered in her eyes. 'Then warn them, Dave. And hope they don't end up like the others. '

She turned to leave. Then paused. Just a second too long. Enough for him to notice. Enough to remember.

He thought of Lisa — of their house in Maryland, with its perfect lawn and cold dinners. A home filled with schedules and silence. A marriage reduced to two intelligence briefings pretending to be people.

For a moment, he wanted to ask Carla to stay. He always did. But guilt spoke louder than longing, and that part of him had been filed away like everything else marked 'need to know.'

The moment passed, like it always did. The door clicked shut behind her.

Ross picked up the secure line and dialled. It rang twice.

'Ellis. Hereford. '

'Brigadier, this is Ross — CIA. I need help in Belize. Something's in motion. Not just cartel. This is coordinated. NATO-grade weapons, mercs, encrypted comms. These aren't locals playing soldier. '

A pause.

'I have just the men,' Ellis said. 'Shaw and Hayes. You know Shaw from Kosovo — reliable, stubborn. The kind of soldier who knows when to keep his mouth shut… and when to burn the world down. '

Ross raised a brow. 'And Hayes?'

'Shaw trusts him,' Ellis said. 'That's not a small thing. '

Ross was quiet for a beat. 'You don't usually gamble on other people's faith. '

'I'm not,' Ellis replied. 'I'm gambling on the part of Shaw that still believes the world's worth saving. And Hayes… he's new. But he's dangerous in the right way. He still believes in lines — and he knows how to cross them. '

A breath. Then: 'Consider it done. I'll brief them personally. '

Ross hung up.

The photo still sat on the desk. The airstrip. The crates. The faint horse mark, half-swallowed by jungle shadow.

He'd seen operations unravel. Agents vanish. Black sites turn red. But this…This felt older.

Shaw and Hayes were the best. But even the best could be swallowed whole by something they didn't see coming. And Ross knew — deep down — that the war against shadows didn't start in Belize.

It began long before Hayes. Before Shaw. Before either man had worn a uniform or buried their first secret.

It began in London.With a man who walked through fire and left echoes behind him.

CHAPTER 1

LONDON, 1980

The townhouse at the end of Westmere Lane looked ordinary — curtained windows, ivy-clad stone, the illusion of peace. Inside, it was war.

Three days ago, six armed insurgents took seventeen hostages. Their demands were exact. Their threats, clearer: one execution per hour until the government complied. Negotiations failed. The Regiment was called in.

William Armitage adjusted the straps of his gas mask, eyes locked on the countdown pulsing at his wrist.

Outside, the wind shifted — the bitter stink of petrol, the electric hum of floodlights cutting through the London mist.

He didn't hear the press. Or the politicians holding their breath. He heard the rhythm. The countdown. The call to move.

'Red One, stand by. ' The voice in his ear was flat. Clinical.

William's pulse stayed steady. He'd rehearsed this breach a hundred times. But tonight, something lingered. Not fear. No doubt. Just focus.

The charge blew. Glass shattered. Smoke surged.

William breached without pause. The hallway exploded — gunfire, screams, choking dust. Shadows flickered in the haze.

He dropped low, MP5 raised. A shape moved in the stairwell — gun lifted. Two rounds. Tight grouping. Target down.

   'One down. '

He flowed forward, slicing doorways and clearing corners. Two SAS troopers ghosted behind him — no words, just silent choreography.

Reflex. Repetition. Rhythm.

On the first landing, another gunman crouched behind a bannister. William ducked, pivoted, and fired through the wood. Blood sprayed the wall.

   'Clear first floor. '

A barricaded room. Four hostages — three women, one man. Blindfolded. Bound. Trembling. Relief washed over them at the sound of boots.

William signalled the medic.

   'Get them out. '

   'Red Four,'

Control's voice cut in. 'Motion — north corridor. '

He moved.

   A door slammed open. A man dragged a hostage into view, pistol jammed to her throat. William didn't blink. Two strides. Gun to the temple. ***Bang.***

   The hostage screamed. William caught her, eyes locking — fear, confusion, relief.

She bolted. He was already gone.

Second floor. Final breach. The door splintered, smoke curling into the dark.

Two shooters.

His pulse didn't quicken. It never did. But tonight felt different.

He fired. One round, chest shot. Clean. First one down.

The second — a brute, wild-eyed — pulled a grenade pin.

And that's when he saw it. A flash of ink, just below the collarbone. Half-hidden by torn fabric. A horse. Rearing. Stylised. Sharp lines. Precise symmetry. Not gang ink. Not homemade. It looked… issued. Branded, not worn. Like it belonged to something larger — an organisation. A creed. The kind of symbol people died for. And killed for.

William didn't hesitate. He drove the man into the wall, hard. The grenade spun loose. William caught it, wrapped it in a fire blanket, and shoved it down the laundry chute. ***Thud.*** The blast shook the walls. Dust rained from the ceiling. And then — silence.

'All clear,' came the call.

William lowered his weapon. The smoke thinned. Every hostage accounted for. Every threat neutralised.

He stood there for a moment. Just one. Not from hesitation — from habit. Making sure it was real. That there was nothing left to kill.

Then he stepped out into the night, black kit soaked with sweat, blood, and soot. The cameras outside caught only the silhouette of a masked man walking through fire. No name. No rank. No hesitation.

But inside Hereford, the story spread by dawn.

First in. Last out.

Seven kills. One grenade. No hesitation.

They didn't call him a hero. Heroes hesitate. They called him a legend.

A man who walked through fire. Unbroken. Untouchable.

More than a soldier. A myth.

CHAPTER 2

NORTHERN LIBYA, 1994

The desert didn't whisper. It waited.

Sergeant Adam Hayes crouched behind a half-buried outpost, NVGs humming, eyes fixed on the dust-choked ridge ahead — a flicker of movement — then stillness again.

His first operation with the Regiment. First-time boots in the sand with the badge on his shoulder. But already, his name carried weight. A reputation built in deeper shadows — brilliant, detached, unorthodox. The sort of man who solved unsolvable problems and didn't flinch when things broke along the way.

Footsteps crunched behind him.

'Hayes?'

The voice had the rough, familiar bark of a soldier who'd seen it all.

Adam didn't turn. 'Yeah. '

The man dropped into cover beside him, dust puffing up from the faded canvas.

'Tony Shaw. They said I was getting a quiet one. Didn't mention you were that Hayes. '

Adam kept scanning. 'Doesn't change the job. '

Tony smirked. 'Fair enough. You really rerouted a Russian strike cell through a weather balloon relay in Turkey?'

'Only half of it was a balloon. '

Tony chuckled. 'Brilliant. '

They were both SAS, but from different bloodlines. Shaw had spent years in Sierra Leone, Bosnia, and sandpits that didn't exist. Hayes was new to the Regiment, but not new to the war.

Their task was simple: rendezvous with a Libyan defector — Farid — who had intel on illegal chemical transfers. In and out. No prints.

Farid arrived late. Sweating. Pale. He handed over a flash drive without eye contact.

'You need to go now,' he said, voice shaking. 'They followed me. '

Adam was about to press him — when the world went to hell.

An RPG slammed into the Land Rover behind them. The blast rolled heat and shrapnel through the checkpoint like a hammer. The concrete cracked. Sand turned to flame.

Gunfire followed — tight, elevated, professional. Not amateurs.

Tony was already moving. 'Three on the ridge! East side!'

He fired in controlled bursts, dropping two before they could adjust. Adam followed, flanking — each round deliberate, every step measured.

Farid stumbled. Adam hauled him behind a flipped chassis as static crackled from the ruined comms unit. Tony dropped beside him, breath ragged, reloading.

'Well, this is well and truly fucked. '

Adam spotted the shattered comms box. Burned. Twisted. But not beyond repair. He flicked open his blade.

'Cover me. '

Tony didn't hesitate — rolled out and laid down fire. A DShK round screamed past, shredding the sandbags an inch from his shoulder.

'Whatever you're doing,' he yelled, 'do it faster!'

Adam's fingers moved fast, stripping wires, rerouting power from the Rover's auxiliary, patching together the remains of a headset into a makeshift field antenna. He tapped a Morse burst into enemy bandwidth. Tight. Fast. Dirty.

Then — chirp. A flicker of light. Signal locked.

Two minutes later, salvation screamed overhead.

At first, it was just pressure — like the desert holding its breath. Then came the thunder.

Twin Apaches ripped through the dark, low and furious, rotor blades carving through smoke and sand. Red strobes pulsed over the battlefield. IR targeting locked on.

The first Hellfire struck the ridge like God's hammer. Flame erupted. The rockface disintegrated. Men vanished mid-step.

Then the chain guns opened up — 30mm cannons shredding the hillside in a brutal crescendo. Enemy tracers flared in panic — and were chewed out of the sky before they could land.

Another missile screamed in from the flank. The ridge folded inward, collapsing in fire and debris. Screams echoed, cut short, final.

Tony ducked, arm over his face.

'Next time,' he muttered, 'you hack first — then I'll shoot.'

The downwash hit like a wall — scorching wind, sand, and smoke. Like the desert itself was bleeding.

Everything roared. Then… nothing.

Silence.

Not peace.

The silence of something extinguished.

Tony glanced at Adam through the smoke. 'Christ… Armitage would've loved this one. '

Adam didn't reply. He wasn't sure if that was a compliment or a warning.

The checkpoint was gone. The air stank of cordite, oil, and scorched meat.

One of the Land Rover's doors lay smouldering in the branches above.

Tony slumped against a blackened wall, teeth clenched against the pain in his arm. 'Bloody hell,' he breathed.

As the Apaches vanished into the smoke, Adam knelt beside the unconscious Farid. He didn't say anything. Just pressed two fingers to the man's neck.

There was a pulse. Faint, but there.

He closed his eyes a second longer than he needed to. Just long enough to feel the world tilt back into balance. Just enough to remember that the pulse mattered.

Tony dropped onto a rock, exhaling hard. He looked at Adam for a long moment, then offered him a flask.

'That,' he said, 'was bloody close. '

That night, a bond was forged — one built on fire and silence. It would be tested, tempered, and reforged again through the years.

They worked the world's harshest fronts — from Middle Eastern deserts to Belfast alleyways.

Adam was the quiet one.

Tony, the spark.

Together, they made chaos work.

As a team, they embodied the creed they'd earned.

Who Dares Wins.

BELFAST — LATER

Adam wiped the sand from his boots as the dust of Libya faded into the recesses of his mind.

He didn't need to look back. The desert's harshness had been a constant.

But Belfast…Belfast was a different war.

Quiet. Cold. A battle fought with words — and whispers.

CHAPTER 3

BELFAST DOCKS, LATE 1994

The ferry groaned against the dock as morning mist clung to the cranes. Diesel hung thick — salt, rust, and the slow decay of steel. The contrast was unmistakable. Libya's heat, chaos, and gunfire had given way to Belfast's damp, oppressive silence.

Adam Hayes crouched behind a concrete pylon, eyes fixed on the gangway. His hand rested on his pistol, but it wasn't the weapon he trusted most — it was the silence. The city's hum was a different kind of noise. Quiet, but heavy. Watching. Beside him, Tony Shaw sparked a battered Zippo to life, lighting his face briefly before vanishing behind a cupped hand.

'Still coming in by ferry?' Tony muttered, smoke threading from his lips.

Adam didn't look at him. 'Home Office man. Carroway. Straight off the Liverpool boat. '

Tony scanned the foggy perimeter, his eyes sharp. 'Place is crawling. Six RUC. One twitchy plain-clothes near the customs shed. '

Adam adjusted his earpiece, voice steady. 'Carroway's in the Jag. Diplomatic plates. We shadow him to the Europa. No stops. No diversions. '

The ferry ramp slammed down with a steel-clanging thud, snapping Adam's attention back to the job.

The black Jaguar rolled off through the fog, flanked by two unmarked cars. Behind them, a disguised blue Ulsterbus followed, suspension sagging under the weight of hidden armour. Two camouflaged pigs idled near the customs lane, diesel smoke curling into the grey.

Tony squinted. 'Rolling pigs? Thought this was supposed to be low-key. '

Adam didn't answer. He was already moving, calculating the next steps. Their job was simple: watch, follow, and keep Carroway safe. But in Belfast, there was always another layer. Another game — just out of sight.

They intercepted the convoy at the loading bay. Carroway looked red-faced and overdressed, like a man already regretting the trip.

Adam stepped in, calm and deliberate. 'Sir. You're in the centre vehicle. No stops. Keep your head down. Eyes open. '

Carroway blinked, uncomfortable. 'Am I armed?'

'No. That's our job. Keep your head down. '

Tony opened the Montego's rear door. Carroway climbed in without a word, and Adam slid into the front left, scanning the streets, watching for any shift in the pattern.

The convoy moved through Belfast's grey maze, quiet and coiled. Adam's eyes flicked across the streets — grey concrete, shuttered shops, old iron fences. The thick air pressed down. The city was different from Libya. Here, the battle was fought in silence. In shadows.

Loyalist murals glared down like sentinels, their eyes following the Montego as it moved past. The weight of the city was everywhere. Watching. Calculating.

Near Divis Street, Adam saw it.

'Tail. Four back. Vauxhall Cavalier. '

Tony glanced in the mirror. 'Too neat. Tail's not twitchy enough. '

'Not RUC. The headlights are wrong. '

'Peel off on Durham. Let's see if they fancy a closer look,' said Adam.

Carroway shifted in his seat, eyes scanning the murals outside the customs window. 'I didn't think they still painted them,' he murmured.

Adam didn't respond.

The Montego veered off the main road, slipping between warehouses and down a narrow backstreet. They couldn't afford to be seen — or give the tail a chance to confirm their suspicions.

The Cavalier followed.

Adam's instincts sharpened. His fingers brushed the Browning in his holster as the car slowed to a stop.

He was out before the vehicle was fully parked, fast, silent, his breath steady as he moved to the rear of the

Cavalier. He slammed a shoulder into the door. It opened with a creak.

'Engine off. Hands where I can see them. '

Three inside. Two young. One older. The older man raised a badge before Adam could speak.

'Special Branch,' he said calmly. 'We had orders to shadow. Contingency detail. '

Adam didn't lower the Browning. His voice was ice.

'Next time, clear it with command. You tail us blind again, I'll write you up as Provos with stolen plates. '

The officer nodded once. He didn't argue.

Adam turned, his eyes narrowing on the alley ahead. Something was off — a shift in the city's rhythm. A subtle signal that things would change again.

The city had survived it all — bombs, bullets, betrayals. The world around them had shifted, but Belfast had its own beat. And now, Adam Hayes was just one of the many shadows moving through it.

But some shadows stayed longer.

LATER THAT NIGHT

Adam's superiors had likened him to William Armitage. Not the man — the myth. The name was whispered in mess halls and scribbled in the margins of mission briefs.

It was the one they brought up when things got ugly and someone muttered, 'Armitage handled worse. '

But Adam didn't believe in ghosts. Not really. He knew the Regiment didn't talk about why Armitage left. Just that one day, he was gone — no medals, no funeral, no plaque. Just a blank space where the man used to be.

Whatever had ended it… It wasn't a failure. It wasn't paperwork. It was something else.

Adam's breath caught in the still night air. The city felt like it was holding its breath, waiting to exhale. And then it did. A distant blast. Sharp. Followed by the long wail of sirens.

Same city. Same scars. Different men. Same war.

CHAPTER 4

They met in the back of a converted textile warehouse off Falls Road — disused, unofficial, the kind of place not listed in parliamentary schedules or RUC logs.

The windows were painted shut. Two portable heaters buzzed against the cold, doing nothing.

The room stank of boiled coffee, damp stone, and resignation. A folding table. Three mismatched chairs. Four men. Carroway, in a rain-dark suit that clung to him like guilt. Opposite, a loyalist representative with a tired face and a scar that made his eye twitch when he smiled. Two others stood in shadow — observers or handlers. UDA, probably. Or something worse.

A heavy envelope lay open on the table.

'You came light,' the loyalist said.

His voice was measured, Ulster-born, but scraped raw by decades of fire.

'I came with what was agreed,' Carroway replied.

His voice didn't tremble. Not yet.

The loyalist lifted the envelope, thumbed through the pages, then laid it flat. A shipment manifest — *South Africa, 1988*. Freight routes. Smuggled crates. Disguised calibres. The kind of document that should no longer exist.

'So you knew,' the loyalist said.

Carroway's jaw flexed. 'I knew men who did. Vega handled the clearance. Tarlen ran the channels. '

The loyalist smiled thinly. 'And the Libyans?'

'Vega handled them too. It was all unofficial. Deniable.
'

'Convenient. '

Carroway exhaled through his nose. 'Effective. At the time. '

The loyalist leaned forward.

'See, here's what we remember. You let us flood this city with weapons, as long as the right names stayed off the ledger. You let South African crates cross the Irish Sea because you needed leverage. Against both sides. To keep balance. Or to make sure it never ended. '

He pulled out a creased photo. Black-and-white. Grainy. A younger man in an arid compound, surrounded by stacked munitions. No insignia. British camo. The face turned slightly, but the build, the posture — *unmistakable.*

'Armitage. London. 1980. Terror standoff. Your people said it was an isolated cell. But now it looks connected. '

Carroway didn't confirm it. He didn't need to.

'We're not here to revise history,' he said. 'We're here to keep it from repeating. '

'Then explain this. '

The loyalist slid a piece of crate stencilling across the table. Torn, charred at one edge. The lines weren't random. They weren't scorched by accident. They were burned deliberately. Stylised. Symmetrical.

A crude horse emblem. Rearing. Faded.

Carroway frowned. He'd seen the shape once before, years back. A debrief photo from a botched op in Lebanon. Same horse. Same pose. Different war.

'Found that burned into a weapons cache south of the border. Last month. '

Silence.

'Your ghosts aren't buried. They're trading again. '

The loyalist stood. 'So either your people have lost control of your contractors… or you never had it. '

He turned and walked out. The observers followed.

Carroway sat still. Then he gathered the manifest, the photo, the charred crate scrap. Tucked them into the envelope.

His hands trembled slightly as he buttoned his coat. Not from cold. From memory. Because some truths didn't stay classified — they just waited.

OVERWATCH —
ROOFTOP, 200 YARDS EAST

Adam watched through the spotting scope, breath clouding the cold night air. Tony lay beside him, rifle cradled, scanning the perimeter.

'Looks like our boy's got company,' Tony muttered.

Adam didn't answer. He kept eyes on the window — Carroway's stillness, the way the loyalist leaned just a little too close.

'You ever seen a spook sweat before?'

'No,' Adam said. 'Not until now. '

A beat passed. Carroway stood.

Tony lowered his scope. 'Meeting's over. Time to roll. '

Adam kept watching a moment longer. Saw the loyalist pocket something small. Then he stood, brushing frost from his sleeves.

'Convoy sets off at 02:14,' he said.

Behind them, Belfast held its breath. In a city built on scars, even silence had a signature. And tonight, it was starting to hum again.

CHAPTER 5

TWELVE YEARS EARLIER — BARCELONA

A decade before, far from the cities where soldiers watched and waited, another kind of awakening was beginning — one not born of war, but memory.

The fire in Hendrik Vega's study had long since died, but the coals glowed like eyes under ash.

Silas moved silently across the Persian rug, avoiding the creaky boards he'd memorised over months. Twelve years old and already practised in silence.

He wasn't sneaking for mischief. He was hunting the truth.

He found the drawer.

It was locked — brass-rimmed, ancient. But the heat had warped the wood slightly. Silas slid a nail file from his sleeve and eased it into the crack. It took time — long minutes of patient, meticulous wriggling.

When it finally popped open, the sound was barely a breath.

Inside: oilskin-wrapped leather, tied with red twine.

Visions of the Stars.

He untied it with reverence.

The parchment inside was brittle and brittle-sweet with the scent of clove and mildew. Diagrams swirled across the pages — planetary alignments, mathematical lattices, magnetic field notations that seemed beyond current science.

Then he turned a page and froze.

The Four Horsemen rode through its illustrations, each entwined with planetary glyphs and strange equations. They were not myth, but mechanisms — forces awakened at thresholds. A cycle encoded in orbit, mass, and memory.

Between the symbols lay fragments — references to the Seven Seals, not as divine judgments, but as planetary alignments: triggers that influenced gravitational fields, solar harmonics, and resonance thresholds.

The Seals were not locks. They were harmonic gates. Fail-safes designed to reset planets — first Mars, now Earth.

A spiral, jagged and asymmetric, burned into the vellum. Not ink. Blood. Dried, blackened — yet vibrant, as if the act that made it had never ended.

He reached out and touched it.

It thrummed. Not metaphorically.

It hummed through his fingertips. Like resonance.

'Silas!'

His father stood in the doorway, coat still damp with rain, eyes like burnished iron. Hendrik Vega's voice was quiet, but the air around him seemed to harden.

'You're not ready. '

Silas closed the book. Not in shame, but defiance.

'Why hide it?'

'Because knowledge is a tide. It lifts the patient and drowns the impulsive. '

Hendrik crossed the room in two strides. He reached for the book.

Silas pulled it away. 'This belongs to me. '

The slap was sharp, but not cruel. A correction, not a punishment.

'That mark wasn't meant for you,' Hendrik said quietly. 'Not yet.'

Silas stood his ground. His cheek burned, but his voice held firm.

'Then why does it sing to me?'

Hendrik didn't answer. He stared at the spiral like it had betrayed him.

'One day,' Silas whispered, almost to himself, 'I'll rewrite it in fire. '

CHAPTER 6

FALLS ROAD – 02:14

The silence in Belfast was never clean. It was tension with a heartbeat. Static wrapped in smoke. Streetlights flickered in sodium haze, casting soft gold over slick tarmac. Somewhere behind it all, a dog barked — sharp, repetitive. It didn't stop. Rain whispered across rooftops and ran down brick walls like blood too tired to flow.

The Ulsterbus was the decoy — painted blue, suspension reinforced, glass retrofitted with armour. Its real cargo wasn't soldiers or civilians. It was Carroway. And tonight, it was rolling him out of Belfast before the fallout caught fire.

Adam Hayes crouched behind a butcher's van, the bonnet still steaming. Rain trickled down his neck. He didn't flinch. Beside him, Tony Shaw wiped his lenses, then raised the binoculars again.

Across the road, Roarke's Bar pulsed with warmth — music thudding through the windows, voices raised in stubborn defiance of everything outside. Civilians laughed. Glasses clinked. Fragile peace danced in the dark.

Tony's voice was low, certain. 'Four lads. Civilian jackets. No comms. One's pacing. '

'GAA crest?'

'Red Hand of Tyrone. Same lad from the docks. '

Adam's breath slowed. 'PIRA logistics. They're not casing the bar. '

Tony nodded. 'They're planting. '

Adam's reply was already movement.

They slid through bins, crates, and back walls slick with moss. Rain soaked their cuffs, their boots, and their breath. The air pressed down, heavy and thick. Every movement had weight.

Then — the sound.

Thump.

Not fire. Worse. A pressure wave. Low and fast.

It hit the chest first, then the ears.

Roarke's wall bowed. Bricks cracked. Glass exploded outward like shrapnel.

A window vented. Then the screams — real, jagged, raw.

Alarms overlapped. Sirens kicked in.

Tony was up. 'Secondary team — there!'

Two shapes burst from the alley — one with an AR-15, the other gripping a sawn-off like a club.

Adam dropped behind a Peugeot. Sighted. Fired. Two rounds. Tight. Clean.

The rifleman folded, gun clattering to the road.

Tony flanked left, fast and silent. He tossed a flashbang.

Pop. Whiteout. Shockwave.

The second man staggered. Tony struck — blade, knee, elbow. Flesh to concrete. Done.

As the Ulsterbus turned the corner, Adam looked back. The bar's front was a scorched wound. Somewhere inside, someone was still screaming.

Adam moved to the downed shooter. The man's chest was slick with blood. Still breathing. Barely. But smiling.

'You're not ours,' the man rasped.

'No. '

'Then you've no idea what's coming. '

Adam stared at him. 'Try me. '

But the man was already gone.

CONVOY — SIMULTANEOUSLY

As smoke spread across Roarke's, another operation was already in motion.

The Ulsterbus extraction rolled quietly through narrow roads. Its paint was sun-faded blue, windows yellowed with grime. A relic — until you saw the suspension. The reinforced plates. The armoured heart beneath the disguise.

Inside, Carroway sat hunched, his briefcase clutched like a lifeline. His tie was askew, his face clammy with fear. Around him, two operatives and a medic scanned every street through slit windows. The corporal crouched in the footwell, radio pressed tight, scanning rooftops.

'Approaching Clonard Gardens,' the driver muttered.

'Stay on fallback,' the corporal snapped. 'No contact from Hayes or Shaw. '

Rain lashed the windshield. The city blurred into dripping shapes. A passing lamp revealed terraced houses, shuttered shops, and satellite dishes rusting in silence.

Then, a van parked wrong.

Headlights flashed once. Twice. *A code.*

The driver took the turn. The bus eased into the junction.

Then: crack. One sharp shot. Close.

This wasn't a firefight. This was an ambush.

Someone knew. Not locals. Not random. A message — before he crossed the water.

'Sniper!' the corporal shouted. 'Keep moving!'

The driver hesitated. Stopped — then the bus jolted forward, too slowly.

Sitting targets.

Another shot. Louder.

Gunfire crackled in the distance.

Tony sprinted toward it, Roarke's fading behind him. Adam, closing fast.

The corporal spun, leaned from the open panel.

There. Rooftop. Movement.

He fired — reflex, trained.

The figure fell.

The bus jerked to a halt.

'Don't stop!' the corporal barked — but too late.

He hit the street running. Boots hit water. Rain fell harder. He reached the body. A girl. Sixteen. Maybe. There was no rifle. No scope. Just rain. A black coat. Jeans and soaked trainers. One shoe had slipped halfway off. Her hand was open. A single pink hairband still looped around her wrist. One heartbeat in the wrong place.

Tony arrived seconds later. Saw the body. Froze.

'Shit. '

Adam appeared at his side.

His silence was louder than gunfire. Something inside him twisted.

The corporal stood frozen, rifle slack in his hands.

'I thought she had something,' he whispered. 'I—I thought…'

He never finished the sentence.

An armoured pig rolled up behind the bus, diesel growling, lights flooding the street. Shadows snapped into shape — guns, uniforms, movement.

'Back on!' someone barked.

The corporal stumbled aboard. The doors slammed. The driver didn't wait this time. The Ulsterbus roared into the mist.

AFTERMATH

The smoke hadn't settled. Not at Roarke's. Not in the alleys. Not in the minds of those who'd seen what shouldn't have happened.

Something had cracked. Not just the wall. Not just the bodies. Something moral. Something human.

Someone would write the report: fog, confusion, a probable crossfire. An acceptable loss in unacceptable times. But every man in that bus would remember. The girl's eyes. The blood in the gutter. The moment the rule was broken. Don't stop.

CHAPTER 7

It tapped against the prefab walls like static, constant, dull, unavoidable. Inside, the heater coughed lukewarm air into a room that smelled of damp wool and scorched coffee. Condensation blurred the windows. A kettle clicked off in the corner. No one moved to pour.

Adam stood still, arms loose at his sides. Plainclothes — black jacket, jeans, boots worn down at the heel. Deliberately unofficial. The rifle stayed locked away. This wasn't a battlefield. It was purgatory.

Tony leaned against the wall, jaw tight. Blood dried under his fingernails. Neither had slept.

'One civilian dead,' Major Haldane said without lifting his eyes from the file. 'Female. Sixteen. No weapon recovered. '

Adam's voice was calm. 'Third shot hit her. We had unconfirmed sniper fire. Rear alley. Elevated position. '

Haldane flipped a page, unread. 'Press has it already. By noon, it'll be everywhere — 'British Soldier Kills Teenager. ' Headlines write themselves. '

'If Stevens had seen this file, he'd have called it a training exercise. ' He closed the file and set it aside like something toxic. 'RUC's calling it clean. Protocol

33

followed. But upstairs wants a name. Public reassurance. Someone to blame. Someone clean enough to burn. '

Tony scoffed. 'Maybe start with the coward in the reinforced bus. Hid behind bulletproof glass while we bled on the street. '

Adam didn't look up. 'Carroway's job was to leave. Ours was to clean up his mess. '

Haldane exhaled. 'You think I wanted this? My name's on that op. My call. If that footage leaks, it won't be Fort Monagh in the papers — it'll be Derry, '72 all over again. White Paper. Headlines screaming murder. A tribunal looking for someone to burn. '

Adam didn't move. 'She was unarmed. The driver panicked. We can't spin that. '

Tony pushed off the wall. 'You need a name? Take mine. '

Haldane looked up, startled. 'You didn't pull the trigger. '

'No. But don't put it on the kid in the footwell. ' His voice was low now, shaking with something raw. 'We watched her bleed in the street. Don't ask me to pretend we didn't. '

Adam spoke softly. 'We own this. All of it. '

Haldane exhaled through his nose. Long. Heavy. 'You understand what that means. '

'Yeah,' Tony said. 'Means we don't walk away. '

Silence. It lingered like smoke.

Haldane stood and crossed to the window. Outside, a pig rumbled past in the grey wash of morning. Tyres hissed in the rain, fading into the distance.

'You're off the street. Both of you. Temporary reassignment. Let the heat pass. '

Adam gave a single nod. 'Understood. '

Haldane turned. Something flickered in his eyes — respect, maybe. Or guilt.

'You two don't play the political game. '

Tony managed a thin smile. 'Not why we signed up. '

'No,' Haldane said. 'But it's why you'll still sleep at night. '

Outside, the sky softened from iron to ash, and rain kept falling.

Somewhere, a mother woke to silence—to the space her daughter used to fill.

And in a prefab office on the edge of a forgotten war, two men stood in the cold, trying to shoulder what couldn't be carried — because no one else would.

CHAPTER 8

HEREFORD – ONE WEEK LATER

Seven days since Belfast. Since the rooftop. Since the girl's hand slipped open and never closed again.

Rain threaded the slate roofs of Stirling Lines, steady and cold.

Inside the barracks, Adam sat alone, headphones in, posture still, the outside world drowned beneath layers of sound. Bach's Passacaglia in C Minor surged in his ears, each movement cutting through static. Not for peace. For precision. He didn't use music to escape. He used it to think. To slice through the noise. It had started years ago, though he rarely let the memory surface.

* * *

A classroom in South Yorkshire — rain on the windows, the smell of chalk and damp coats.

Mrs. Laughton had wheeled in the cassette player again. Said it was discipline in sound.

The others laughed. He didn't.

The cello line had wrapped around him like armour.

Something about the structure — unbreakable, exact — stuck fast in his bones.

He hadn't known what it was called, not then.

But years later, he'd hunted it down. Bach. The same one.

Now he played it before missions — not for comfort, but to build walls inside his mind.

Sharp. Unyielding. Clean.

Violence, order, decision — they all followed rhythm. By the time the last note fell silent, Adam was already moving.

✳ ✳ ✳

The briefing room was sharp with fluorescent light and the stale bitterness of coffee long since burned. He and Tony sat across a worn mahogany table — civilian clothes, soldier's bearing. One silent. One coiled like a wire.

Tony drummed a fingertip rhythm on his knee, but even that fell quiet when the door opened.

Brigadier Ellis entered first — broad-shouldered, silver-haired, with eyes that had seen too many cleanup reports.

Behind him came a stranger: government-issue, Barbour trench coat, polished brogues, and that quiet arrogance found only in corridors of power.

'Gentlemen,' the man said, offering a hand. 'Secretary Blake. I've read your file. All of it. '

Adam rose but didn't shake — just a curt nod.

Tony accepted the handshake with a half-smile that didn't reach his eyes.

Blake turned to Ellis. 'They did it right. Held the line. Didn't flinch. And didn't lie. '

Ellis nodded once. 'They never do. '

Blake leaned in, lowering his voice. 'Something is moving. Mainland-based. Off-record. Unofficial. But when the call comes, I need people I can count on. Men who don't blink. '

'That your version of a job offer?' Tony muttered without humour.

'Call it an invitation,' Blake replied. 'For later. When the politics get worse. '

Adam's voice was quiet steel. 'We didn't do it for favours. '

'Exactly why I'm here,' Blake said.

Ellis didn't raise his voice. 'Sir, with respect — deploying Shaw and Hayes again this soon is a risk. Optics aren't exactly clean after Belfast. '

Blake barely glanced up. 'Optics don't win wars. Men like them do. '

Ellis held his ground. 'Until one of them ends up on the front page. '

Blake closed the file. 'Then let's make sure it's for the right reasons. '

He slid two plain envelopes across the table.

Inside: MOD commendations. Dated. Signed. Clean.

'Don't frame it,' Blake added, already turning to leave. 'Just remember, someone knows what you're worth. '

The door closed with a quiet click.

Ellis stayed silent for a beat, then exhaled. 'You're off the board for a month. Let the press cycle fade. After that, back to tasking. '

Tony stretched like he'd just defused a bomb with his teeth.

They lingered side by side, boots planted in silence.

Outside, the rain kept falling, but it felt different now —not softer, just less wrong.

Whatever came next, they'd face it side by side.

And in the back of Adam's mind, the music played on — not a balm, but a signal.

A warning wrapped in rhythm.

CHAPTER 9

SHEFFIELD – PRESENT DAY

The engine rattled low, idling outside a distribution depot near Doncaster. Rain smeared the windscreen, and the wipers barely kept up. The amber glow of a forecourt light buzzed against the cold.

John Goodman sat behind the wheel of a Volvo FH16, hands resting at ten and two. It was the exact grip he used to use on a rifle. Different weight. Same ghosts.

He wore a fleece zipped to the chin and a Sheffield Wednesday beanie pulled low. Thirty-seven now. Still lean. He still kept his boots clean. But the uniform was long gone.

He'd left the Regiment eighteen years ago. Quietly. No ceremony. No badge. Just an honourable discharge and a file no one talked about.

He didn't talk about it either.

He didn't have to.

1994 – FORT MONAGH BARRACKS
FOUR DAYS AFTER THE ROOFTOP

Adam Hayes stood outside the medical block, collar turned up against the wind. His boots were soaked.

The door buzzed once and clicked open. No escort.

Inside, the lighting was low, one nurse on rotation. The RMP officer by the door didn't speak — just nodded once. Respect or pity. Hard to say.

John Goodman sat on the edge of the cot, face grey and hollow. He was still in uniform, shirt rumpled; one sleeve rolled to the elbow where a nurse had taken blood. His hands didn't stop moving — thumb over thumb, again and again.

He didn't look up when Adam entered.

Adam sat in the folding chair opposite. Silence hung between them. Not heavy. Not awkward. Just real.

Finally, John spoke.

'She didn't even run. '

Adam nodded once. 'I know. '

John's voice cracked. 'I thought... I thought she had something in her coat. A barrel. A device. She twitched, and I—I didn't mean...'

He trailed off.

'They told me it was clean. RUC says it was justified. But I saw her face, Adam. I see it every night. It doesn't matter what they write down. '

Adam didn't correct him. There was nothing to fix.

'You ever kill someone who didn't deserve it?' John asked, not as a challenge, just a question a man asks when he's broken.

Adam looked him in the eye. 'Yes. '

John finally met his gaze. 'Does it stop hurting?'

41

Adam said nothing.

The room buzzed with low light. The RMP officer didn't move. The nurse didn't look over.

Adam stood after ten minutes. Didn't offer words — just a hand.

John took it.

Yorkshire boys. Different cities. Same weather.

Same ghosts.

* * *

SHEFFIELD – PRESENT DAY (2013)

John backed the lorry into bay five like he'd done a thousand times. Precision. No room for error. The spotter gave him a thumbs-up.

He climbed down, his boots splashing into a puddle. He lit a cigarette under the eaves and watched steam curl from the bonnet.

Sometimes, on the longer hauls, the roads went quiet. Too quiet. And he'd hear it again — the crack of the shot. The way the girl's coat moved. The way the driver didn't stop the bus.

He'd kept the clipping. He still had it in his glove box. British Soldier Shoots Civilian Girl in Belfast Riot.

They never printed his name. But it was his all the same.

His missus left him four years back. Said he'd gone hollow. Maybe he had.

But he never raised his voice. Never drank past two. Never let a single load shift in the trailer.

He lived clean.

Because he knew what dirty looked like.

LATER

Sometimes, he'd catch himself scanning rooftops when pulling into city centres. Sometimes he'd wake with his hands clenched into fists, heart pounding, breath shallow. But mostly, he just drove. And sometimes — on the rarest nights — he remembered the quiet voice of Adam Hayes in that Belfast ward.

No judgment.

No salvation.

Just two Yorkshiremen sitting with something that couldn't be lifted.

CHAPTER 10

1984 — ARMITAGE RESIDENCE
LATE AFTERNOON

The light was thinning, stretched long and low across the back fields. William Armitage stood at the sink, rinsing the last traces of oil and solvent from a battered mess tin. The silence in the house was deep enough to catch the soft pop of the cooling tap.

He was between deployments—five days at home, if the winds held.

Claire sat nearby, curled into one of the old dining chairs, head down over a notebook. She was twelve— maybe thirteen—but already sharper than most adults he knew. She hadn't asked about the rifle on the side table. She didn't need to.

A shift in the air pulled his attention sideways. Outside.

He moved to the front window. A black car had stopped by the gate. Clean. Unmarked. Parked with precision. No dust on the tyres. No hesitation in the approach.

William dried his hands on the towel and stepped out onto the gravel. The door clicked shut behind him with a sound that felt final.

The man at the gate was tall, neat. Civilian clothes, but not a civilian posture. His gaze held weight. Like he'd already seen what came next.

'Sergeant Armitage,' the man said calmly.

William didn't reply.

The man held out a small, black card. Matte finish. Embossed only with a single symbol: a stylised horse in motion, its head turned back, surrounded by seven faint arcs—like planetary rings collapsing out of step.

'I'm not here to threaten you,' the man said. 'And I'm not recruiting. '

William remained still, arms folded. 'Then speak fast. '

The man nodded slightly.

'Sarajevo wasn't supposed to be remembered. Not the real part. Not what you saw. ' He studied William's reaction. 'But someone remembered it. And someone noticed you did too. '

A pause. Measured. Intentional.

'You've seen the signs. Repeats that don't behave like coincidence. Signals inside signals. '

William's voice was low. 'Who sent you?'

'No one I answer to,' the man said. 'Not a threat. Just a reading. You've seen the pressure building. '

He nodded toward the house—too casually.

'The girl… she's bright. Too bright. If she starts to draw connections, you may not be able to stop it. '

William stepped forward. Controlled. Calm. And deadly clear.

'Mention my daughter again, and you'll be in that ditch behind you before your next breath. '

The man didn't flinch. Just nodded once, like he expected that.

'I'm not here to start anything,' he said. 'Just to remind you—some truths weren't buried. They were planted. '

He turned without another word, walked back to the car, and drove off into the dusk. William watched until the lights were gone. Then stood a while longer, listening to the silence that returned.

Inside, Claire looked up from the table.

'Was that someone from your work?'

'No,' William said. 'Not exactly. '

He turned, checked the windows, and locked the door. That night, after the house went quiet, he went to the shed.

He laid out the old rope. Checked the compass. Reset the weight on the packs. He hadn't done that in years.

And before first light, when Claire came outside rubbing sleep from her eyes, he handed her a blade and said nothing at all.

Because he didn't believe in prophecy.

But he believed in pattern.

And something was waking again.

CHAPTER 11

TRIPOLI, LIBYA – 1987

The safehouse sat tucked behind a rusted gate and a diplomatic lie. Officially vacant, it still drew power from the Italian grid and water from a sealed cistern. Unmarked vehicles came and went. No flags flew. No questions were asked.

William Armitage arrived alone. He'd been briefed to expect a formal check-in—a routine consultation on weapons flow data tied to the Armagh corridor. Just oversight. Confirm logistics, assess deniability, and leave quietly.

They didn't send a diplomat because a diplomat might ask the wrong questions. They didn't send intelligence— too traceable. They sent Armitage—a soldier in plain clothes. Someone who could see the fault lines but wouldn't leave a paper trail when they cracked.

But the moment he crossed the threshold, he knew it wasn't oversight. It was something else. Something already moving without him.

Inside, the tiles were cool, the air dead. A newspaper lay folded on a chair by the door. The headline, French, peeked out beneath the ink-stained page: Weapons Seized Off Brittany – Suspected Libyan Link.

A man stood near the far wall, sleeves rolled, tie loosened, a file open on a plain steel table.

'Sergeant Armitage,' he said. 'Appreciate your punctuality. '

'Didn't think I had a choice. '

The man extended a hand. Armitage ignored it.

'Tarlen,' he said. 'I liaise between foreign operations and internal modelling. You've been in Belfast. You understand the dynamics. '

'No,' Armitage said. 'I understand when something stinks. And this stinks. '

Tarlen gave a faint smile. 'We're containing volatility. That's all. Tension maintains structure. Without it, you get collapse. '

Armitage looked him over. 'You talk like a man who's never had to clear the bodies afterwards. '

Tarlen motioned to the table. 'Read the file. '

Armitage flipped through the manifest. Valletta, Durban, Luanda. Then paused.

'You routed this through Valletta?'

Tarlen nodded, too casually.

'The corridor's dead, or it's supposed to be. Last time Armscor crates moved through Valletta, they ended up in Savimbi's camps. Coast wasn't even dry yet—nerve agents, bio sludge, apartheid's last science fair. '

Tarlen offered a thin smile. 'Old routes. New uses. '

'No,' Armitage said. 'Old fingerprints. Same mess. '

'We manage thresholds. It's not about weapons. It's about equilibrium. '

Armitage closed the folder with a flat slap.

'Equilibrium? While the Libyans flood both ends of the line?'

Tarlen shrugged. 'They're opportunists. We're planners. '

'No,' Armitage said. 'You're gamblers. With other people's lives. '

Tarlen leaned back. 'Violence isn't chaos. It's a pattern. You just need distance to see it. '

'You think that makes it noble?'

'I think it makes it manageable. '

Armitage's voice dipped. 'I've seen the name Carroway on some of those manifests. If he's signing off, he knows more than he wants to admit. '

'Carroway signs what he's told to sign. That's his strength. '

Armitage shook his head. 'That kind of strength breaks things. '

Tarlen studied him. 'The corridor holds. '

'For now. Until it doesn't. '

Tarlen said nothing.

'You want metaphors? Fine. It's like tuning a wire. Too much slack and nothing moves. Too much tension, and it snaps. You call that balance?'

'Yes. I do. '

Armitage stepped back from the table. 'I've lost men in corridors like this. You sit here and name it theory. I name it collateral. '

Tarlen watched him without blinking.

He reached the door. Paused.

'There are things you can control. But not everything. If this spirals—and it will—don't say you weren't warned. '

He stepped into the heat, jaw set, heart already moving three steps ahead. A siren wailed in the distance.

Tarlen stood alone, unmoving. The quiet around him wasn't stillness. It was waiting—like the pattern was deciding what to do next.

Somewhere behind his eyes, the pattern was still forming.

CHAPTER 12

BALKANS – 1988

The rain came down hot, thick with the stink of cordite, sweat, and diesel.

William Armitage moved through the ruined village like a blade through smoke. The op had been planned as ghost work—four men, one target. Intercept a rogue arms convoy smuggling NATO ordnance to paramilitary groups too dirty for the alliance to name.

The convoy never arrived.

The ambush did.

A trip flare cracked overhead. Then came the gunfire —short, disciplined bursts from rooftops and crumbling doorways.

'Contact!' someone shouted—probably Steve.

Dan 'Doc' Halliday was already pulling cover near a collapsed wall. Steve Manning returned fire from the far side of the road. One trooper went down in the opening seconds.

Armitage didn't blink.

'Left flank—two up! Suppress and move!'

He pushed Manning forward and peeled right, MP5 at the shoulder, slicing through doorways with practised precision. His heartbeat never rose. There was no fear—just rhythm. Just the job.

A figure darted across the alley—young, small, holding something long.

Armitage didn't fire.

A stick. Just a boy. Not a threat. He didn't fire. But something stayed with him anyway.

Then came the blast.

The RPG struck the archway ten metres ahead. The pressure wave slammed him sideways into stone, burying him in dust and fractured brick. His vision went grey. His mouth filled with blood and copper and dirt. He tried to stand—failed.

Then he looked down.

His left leg was gone below the knee.

Shredded.

Boot missing. Bone exposed. Blood pulsing in sharp arterial bursts.

He reached for his belt and wrapped it high around his thigh. Cinched it tight. Passed out for a second.

Came back.

Keyed his mic with shaking fingers.

'Red One down. Heavy bleeding. Hostile contact sector five. '

'Copy. Evac inbound. Hold tight. '

Footsteps in the dark.

Armitage dragged himself behind a half-collapsed wall. Raised his sidearm.

Two silhouettes.

He waited for the angle.

Fired—three shots. One dropped.

The second raised a weapon and clipped him in the shoulder.

Armitage fired again.

Two to the chest. One to the face.

Silence.

He dropped the mag. Slapped in a fresh one. Fingers slick with blood.

Then Halliday was there—eyes wide, grabbing him under the arms, dragging him back into the shadows.

'You're hit!'

Armitage didn't respond.

Didn't need to.

He held until the bird arrived, half-conscious, half-dead.

And just before it took him, he saw it—across the fractured wall, half-lit by firelight:

A horse, rearing, sketched in black charcoal.

Around it, a ring of seven stars.

He'd seen it before—hadn't he?

Old. Marked. Waiting.

And then everything went black.

CHAPTER 13
THE PRINCESS MARY'S HOSPITAL, RAF AKROTIRI

CYPRUS. TWO WEEKS LATER

William Armitage woke to antiseptic air and the quiet hum of filtered light. The ceiling above him was white, institutional, and very still.

The nurse had soft hands and a voice made for bad news.

'You're lucky,' she said. 'You kept your life. '

He turned his head. Looked down. The blanket was smooth where his leg used to be.

'You'll walk again,' she told him. 'There are options. Rehabilitation. The Regiment looks after its own. '

He didn't answer. She left quietly.

He stared at the ceiling for another hour.

Didn't ask about his team. Didn't ask for a medal. Didn't ask what came next. ***He already knew.***

Margaret arrived on a military flight from London, their daughter Claire beside her, seventeen, sharp-eyed, trying not to look afraid.

They spent an hour at William's bedside. No tears. Just the weight of what was lost, and the fragile hope of what might still be rebuilt.

That afternoon, needing air, Margaret suggested they get away. Something ancient. Something still standing.

They drove west to Kolossi Castle.

The limestone keep rose pale and proud under the Cypriot sun. Inside, the air was cool and dry. The stones held old things—oaths, prayers, blood. Buried deep.

Margaret wandered through the lower hall, reading plaques. Claire drifted ahead, drawn through a narrow archway into a small, half-forgotten chapel. And stopped.

On the far wall, a fresco. Faded by time, sun, and smoke. The Crucifixion—simple, almost primitive. Christ hung bowed. Mary and John stood hollow-eyed. At their feet, a dark mound—Golgotha. Beneath the cross, nearly hidden: a fleur-de-lis.

Claire stepped closer. Something felt… wrong.

'The halos,' she murmured. 'They're aligned. '

Margaret entered behind her. 'What do you mean?'

'They form a triangle. Perfectly spaced. That's not artistic coincidence. It's deliberate. '

Margaret peered at the faded figures. 'You think it's symbolic?'

Claire nodded, eyes tracing invisible lines. 'Not just symbolic. Structural. Ratio. Pattern. '

Something stirred. Not grief. Not faith. A question she couldn't yet form. Redemption. Cycles. The repetition of sacrifice. She didn't know it yet, but this was the moment that would shape her life.

This fresco. This geometry.

This subtle break in the expected.

It wasn't just art. It was a signal.

Years later, she would study redemptive cycles in religious iconography at the Smithsonian. She would decode ancient symbolic systems at the Warburg Institute. She didn't want to believe.

She wanted to understand. But it began here.

In a quiet Cypriot chapel.

In the shadow of her father's silence.

With a triangle of halos, a buried skull, and a whisper in the stone.

✱ ✱ ✱

That evening, back at the hospital, Claire sat beside William's bed. The air was cooler now. Heavy with unspoken things.

'There was a painting,' she said quietly.

William didn't look at her. His eyes followed the slow turn of the ceiling fan.

'At the castle?'

She nodded. 'A crucifixion. But not normal. There were numbers hidden in the robes. A skull beneath the cross. And a fleur-de-lis—tiny, behind the right hand. '

He was quiet for a long time. Then: 'Some artists weren't painting faith,' he said. 'They were preserving memory. '

She tilted her head. 'You've seen it before?'

His voice dropped. 'That monastery. Outside Sarajevo. Before the IED. '

Claire didn't move.

'There was a diagram under the altar,' William continued. 'Cut into stone. A spiral. Too perfect to be done by hand. Too old to be modern. '

His face changed—hardened.

'The firefight lasted six minutes. The silence started after. '

Claire waited.

'They called it a relic,' he said. 'It wasn't. '

Then, finally:

'It wasn't the blast. It's what's already starting to follow. '

He closed his eyes. And the silence returned.

CHAPTER 14
VATICAN CITY 1990

The door whispered shut behind him. Silas stood alone in the Vatican's restricted archives, the air sharp with age and iron. Rows of lead-lined cabinets loomed like sentinels, each drawer a sealed confession. He didn't flinch. He had been here before—not in place, but in memory.

He'd told Hendrik he was in Vienna. The climate symposium would buy him two days. Just long enough to cross into Rome unnoticed. Just long enough to find what his father had taken from him. There would be no second chance. Hendrik had locked down every known trace of the manuscript. After tonight, there would be no more loopholes. If Silas didn't see the original now, he never would—not until Hendrik was dead.

His father's study had held only fragments. A redacted translation. A faded echo. Silas had been twelve when he'd found it—when the glyph had first stirred something in him that wasn't learned. Back then, the resonance had whispered. Now, it thrummed in his teeth.

He moved without hesitation. Past catalogue alcoves. Down the secondary spine. Left at the arch marked Ordo

Secreta. He no longer needed maps or stolen notes. The layout lived inside him now—as though remembered.

He hadn't come uninvited. He'd written to the Jesuit—two years of silence: formulas, glyphs, harmonic alignments. No reply. But the drawer was unlocked.

Drawer 41–237. Visiones Stellarum.

He paused. His fingertips hovered over the latch. The sigil—an eight-pointed star bisected by a spiral—matched the one he'd stolen years ago from Hendrik's vault. It hadn't aged. Neither had the pull.

He opened the drawer. Inside, vellum sheets rested in a cradle of cedar and cloth. He reached in—not reverently, but with a surgeon's focus—peeling back the top layer.

'Seven-fold symmetry,' he murmured. 'Not decorative. Causal. ' His fingertip traced the arcs. 'Septem… not a number. A structure. '

The first image: seven stars in a harmonic curve—one fractured, disjointed. He exhaled.

The second: a rearing horse, not drawn, but shaped by etched interference—moire lines, ancient and deliberate. Not art. Resonance caught in matter.

The third: a line of half-faded Latin.

Et cum resonantia septima se recludit, apertio—

(And with the seventh resonance, the opening—)

The line broke off. Blank parchment beyond. Gone. Or excised.

He stared until the candlelight bent sideways. The tearing came again—behind his eyes. A pressure not of this world. A red horizon. A city drowned in dust. A man screaming through mirrored corridors as pylons folded in silver flame.

Then—silence.

He steadied himself on the cabinet. The stone beneath his palm felt warm, as if the archive itself remembered.

A voice spoke from behind the shelves—dry, quiet, brittle as ash. 'You've remembered it. '

Silas turned. A thin figure emerged from the shadows. His cassock was worn at the cuffs, his eyes flickering like static caught in glass.

'Who told you I'd come?' Silas asked.

'No one tells,' the priest replied. 'But the archive knows. It exhales when one of you draws near. '

Silas said nothing, lifting the vellum again.

The priest stepped closer, voice low. 'That line wasn't mistranslated. It was never finished. '

'You know what it means?'

'Only as a seismograph knows an earthquake—when it's too late. '

Silas let the vellum fall gently back to its cradle.

'You didn't take it,' the priest observed.

'I can't,' Silas said. 'If I did—he'd know. My father sees more than you think. Perhaps even through your eyes. '

The priest gave a faint nod. 'Good. This isn't meant to be taken. Only remembered. And that page is only a shard. The manuscript runs deeper than this vault. '

'Then why let me see it?'

The priest's gaze held him. 'Because memory outlives possession. And sometimes… memory is sharper. '

Silas studied the page one last time, then closed the drawer—slow, deliberate.

'My name is D'Alverny,' the priest said. 'I filed this record thirty years ago. Encoded it. Buried it. Assigned it to silence. '

'Why?'

D'Alverny's fingers traced the brass edge of the drawer. His voice thinned. 'In 1966, we dismantled the Index Librorum Prohibitorum. Officially: openness. Privately… housecleaning. Dangerous texts weren't burned. Just… set aside. Memory, delayed. '

He looked back at Silas. 'This one nearly burned. I argued otherwise. Some secrets need time, not ash. '

'You believed it?' Silas asked.

'I believed it wasn't yet understood. It's truths… not ready. '

Silas nodded once. No more questions.

He stepped into the shaft of moonlight. The door behind him remained open—its breath held just a moment too long.

CHAPTER 15
QUITO, ECUADOR – 1991

The rain had drowned half the city. Mudslides carved through the hills, dragging homes into the river. Solis watched from a fourth-floor office with a cracked window and a flickering fluorescent light. The square below churned with smoke, tear gas, looted petrol fires, bodies moving like insects beneath floodlight and thunder.

He stood beside a transistor radio, untouched coffee going cold. He wasn't military. Not yet. Just a trade liaison. A political attaché in title. But in this room, they waited for his word.

A man in uniform approached, wet to the elbows.

'Zone 3 has collapsed. They've breached the grain depot. '

'And?'

'Twenty-five wounded. We expect more. '

Solis didn't blink. He turned to the filing cabinet and pulled a sheet marked with import futures and price ceilings. Damp fingerprints smudged the margins. He picked up the phone.

'Increase maise futures by twenty-eight percent. Blame Cuban interference. Tell the Americans the rebels are foreign-backed. '

The officer hesitated. 'And the locals?'

Solis closed the folder. His voice softened—just slightly. 'Let them riot. We'll feed them later. When the IMF is watching. '

A child screamed outside—a thin, raw sound that sliced through the storm. Solis moved to the window. Rain streaked the glass. Below, a woman clawed through a ruptured sack of flour, knees deep in runoff. For a moment, her eyes lifted—met his.

And in that breath, he weighed the cost. Not lives. Leverage.

He shut the blinds. Darkness settled across the room.

'Tell the President,' he said. Quiet now. Certain. 'The riot's over. The economy won. '

CHAPTER 16

BOGOTÁ, COLOMBIA – NIGHT

Rosa couldn't sleep. The rain hadn't stopped in three days, but it wasn't the storm that kept her awake. It was the silence.

Her brother's patrol had vanished outside Meta. No radio. No trace. The official report read like it had been written before they even disappeared. Rebels. Bandits. Routine.

She knew what routine looked like. *This wasn't it.*

She sat on the edge of the hotel bed, elbows on her knees, the flickering lamp throwing uneven light across the floor. Her boots lay by the door, still caked in red mud. The signal had come hours ago—encrypted, buried deep in a relay transmission not meant for civilian eyes. Not a message exactly. A pulse. Patterned. Repeating.

A memory, hidden in noise.

She worked it open instinctively, the way a conservator lifts pigment from fresco. Not code in the traditional sense. Layered—shaped like language, built like sound. Beneath the data mess, something pulsed at fixed intervals.

A spiral.

Seven arcs, coiled like an ancient fingerprint. She'd seen the same pattern scrawled on a wall in San Salvador. On the buttstock of a confiscated rifle in Chiapas. At the border station where her brother's unit had last checked in.

And now here. Again. Woven into the signal.

But this time, something else lived beneath it—metadata, stripped and weathered, from an old U. S. Navy weather surveillance protocol. A ghost in the file header.

VEGA, H.

Rosa's breath caught. Hendrik Vega.

Dutch climatologist. Publicly, a philanthropist and climate theorist. Once a consultant on Vatican environmental policy and high-atmosphere modelling. His work had faded after the mid-eighties, but not in the way legacies fade. He hadn't retired. He had vanished.

No conferences. No papers. His Barcelona estate had shifted quietly into a private foundation. His name was struck from research boards. The last public reference she'd found was from 1987.

Nobody disappears that cleanly unless someone makes sure they do.

And now—here it was again. The same waveform. A resonance pattern first logged by U. S. Naval systems in 1981. Now appearing in encrypted signals. In jungle regions. In the places where people like her brother disappeared.

Same spiral. Same pulse. Same name—buried and rising.

Her fingers hesitated on the laptop. She closed her eyes for a breath longer than necessary.

Javi, if you're out there—

She swallowed it down.

Rosa reached for the envelope she hadn't dared send. Folded and refolded until the edges had worn soft. Inside: copied photos, resonance sketches, and one grainy image pulled from an intercepted border transmission. A young man—blurred, but if you knew where to look, identifiable. A scar near the left eye. Same as the man spotted outside Geneva. Possibly Vega's son.

Her pulse kicked. Who would believe her? The agencies were compromised. Local forces—bought or silenced. Even the NGOs had gone quiet.

One name came back.

Ross. David Ross. She'd met him once, briefly. Analyst? Field liaison? She hadn't been sure. But when she'd mentioned the seven-fold spiral, something in him had shifted. Not confusion—recognition. He'd said nothing. Just scribbled a number on a napkin and walked away.

She scrawled his name across the envelope.

ROSS — Secure Transfer Protocol, Langley Dispatch

A long shot. Maybe pointless. But better than silence.

She stared at the seal a moment longer.

Pressed her palm to it. Then whispered, low, almost a promise— 'Make them remember. '

CHAPTER 17

CAMBRIDGE, 1990: ECHOES BEFORE SIGNAL

The library smelled of dust, ambition, and things meant to be forgotten. Outside, the late autumn rain tapped politely at the high windows, like it had somewhere better to be.

Simon Arkwright adjusted his headphones and leaned further over his notes, half-listening to The Cure bleeding from his Walkman. His left sock had a hole. His mug said 'Rutherford > Bohr. ' He didn't remember where it came from.

Julian Thorne sat cross-legged on the rug, poring over a battered paperback on Cold War diplomacy, a biro in his mouth and an open packet of crisps on his lap. The flat smelled of takeaway korma, damp paper, and heated arguments.

Their flat on Trumpington Street was barely more than a corridor with beds, but it had character. Books stacked in columns by subject. Two desks and one decent chair. A kettle that hissed with defiance and a radiator that worked when threatened.

'You can't honestly believe Kissinger's approach to Vietnam was anything but performative,' Julian said without looking up.

Simon rolled his eyes. 'You eat cereal with a fork. Your takes are invalid. '

Julian gestured with the crisp. 'It's efficient. Leaves the milk. '

'You're unwell. '

They weren't best friends. Not exactly. But they orbited each other—drawn by some shared gravity. Julian with his biting wit and surgical logic. Simon with his technical brilliance and absolute allergy to pretension. Together, they could deconstruct anything: a policy paper, a quantum model, a box of cheap wine.

Julian asked questions no one else dared. Hypotheticals that hung too long in the air.

'If you could reframe history to avoid a war, would it matter if the version was a lie?'

Simon would blink. Think. Frown.

'A lie's still a lie. '

Julian would smile. 'Only if someone remembers the original. '

✳ ✳ ✳

Simon had started poking around systems that shouldn't be open. It began with a mistyped login string in the bursar's database. Then the housing authority's records. Then the transport commission. Not for profit. Not for glory.

'They make rules to protect themselves,' he said one night, eyes flickering with reflected code. 'The more you prod, the more you see the rot. '

Julian watched him with quiet interest. 'And what do you do when you see it?'

Simon cracked a grin. 'Change the rules. '

A week later, the college meal plan system mysteriously refunded every overcharge since 1983.

Julian didn't touch keyboards much. But he watched. And when he spoke, it was with surgical aim.

'People are just algorithms,' he told Simon once. 'They run on fear, reward, and repetition. Interrupt that cycle, and you can rewrite anything. '

Simon snorted. 'You're a lunatic. '

Julian didn't blink. 'I'm curious. '

They were still boys pretending to be men.

Simon missed his sister back home. Julian never spoke about family. They played chess on a board missing two pawns. Replaced them with Monopoly pieces. They made rules. Broke them. Argued about film scores. Left post-it notes on milk cartons with equations or obscure insults.

But cracks were forming.

Julian's hypotheticals grew colder. Less academic. He once drafted a complete student referendum just to see how fast he could polarise a debating society.

Simon started deleting logs from systems he hadn't meant to access. Not out of guilt—but out of instinct.

It still wasn't destiny.

It was boredom. Rain. A hole in the wall. A missing line in a budget file.

Just a question, asked by one friend to another, in a flat with no insulation and too many books.

Before the edits. Before the spiral.

Before Julian Thorne learned how to lie beautifully.

Before Simon Arkwright started trying to fix the world by breaking into it.

***

Some truths are born not in trauma, but in curiosity too sharp to ignore. And some monsters begin not in malice, but in a flatmate's grin, and the sound of rain on glass.

CHAPTER 18
CAMBRIDGE, 1991

The rain didn't just fall that night. It pounded. Hammered. Like it was trying to shake loose something hidden in the bones of the chapel.

Simon Arkwright sat in the window of the flat he shared with Julian Thorne, watching the water blur the lights outside. Inside, the room buzzed with low static from a soldering station left half-running, the smell of burnt copper still clinging to the air.

Julian wasn't back yet. He'd been spending more time off campus lately, disappearing for days, sometimes to Europe. Once, he mentioned Vienna. Or was it Rome? It didn't matter. What mattered was that he was slipping out of orbit. Tonight, he was down in the archives again. Simon always knew where Julian was, even if Julian never said it aloud. Something was shifting in him—subtle, seismic. A rhythm emerging. Quiet. Precise. Relentless. Not unlike Simon's own, but colder. Cleaner. Like a system rewriting itself.

Simon turned back to his laptop, rubbing at his temple. A tangle of windows sat open: fragmented records, server logs, grant allocations. All routes leading nowhere—or more precisely, to something that had been hidden on purpose.

Royston.

That name again.

Julian had found the trial reference. Trial 17-B. Neurogenic Modulation. Buried where no one was supposed to look. Then, in that voice of his—cool, amused, almost lazy:

'You're better with systems. See where the rest of it ends up. '

Simon should have said no. But he didn't. He couldn't.

Two days later, Simon knew more than he wanted to. More than he could explain.

Three test subjects. Two seizures.

One dead.

It wasn't a rumour anymore. It was real. Recorded. Buried. Sanitised. And when he told Julian, his voice a cracked whisper over lukewarm tea, Julian had only smiled. Not kindly. Not triumphantly. Like someone who had already guessed the ending.

Julian submitted the report.

Simon didn't help. Didn't protest either. He watched. Watched as Julian typed each word like it didn't cost him anything. Clinical. Calm. No anger. Just precision.

Simon thought it was bravery.

He was wrong.

72

Three days later, the fallout began.

Julian was reprimanded. Formally. Quietly. Brutally.

Simon wanted to argue. To speak up. But by then, Julian was already folding inward—not hurt, not shaken. Just shifting. Like something inside him had settled into place.

Then came the ceremony.

Royston.

Award. Applause. Champagne.

Simon stood in the back. Not with Julian. Not really with anyone.

He watched the smile on Royston's face and felt something twist.

The system had eaten the truth.

Julian never spoke about it. Not directly.

But Simon saw what came next.

The memo. The forgery. The fire it lit in student forums. The way Julian sat in the corner, eyes scanning headlines, unmoved.

He didn't want justice. He wanted proof that he could bend the system back.

He got it.

Simon should have been proud. Instead, he felt cold.

* * *

The flat got quieter after that. Not in sound. In presence. Julian stopped finishing his sentences.

Simon stopped asking him to.

73

He packed one afternoon without ceremony. Left a note. Then threw it away. What was the point?

Julian didn't ask why. Simon didn't need to say. Because he knew what Julian had learned. That history didn't belong to those who uncovered it. It belonged to those who rewrote it first.

Chapter 19
Kolossi, Cyprus – 1571

The chapel walls cracked as the flames climbed higher. Plaster fell in trembling sheets, each crash echoing like a forgotten bell. Smoke clawed its way up the frescoes, curling them at the edges, lifting paint from stone like skin from bone.

Father Nicodemus stumbled through the nave, robes scorched, fingers blistered from the altar fire. The codex was gone—burned or buried in the rubble beneath the sanctuary vault. The reliquary had ruptured. The seal had broken.

And still the fresco remained.

He turned to face it, coughing against the ash. Even in the smoke, the crucifixion glowed faintly—Christ rigid above a skull, Mary and John weeping at the base, their halos cracked like broken suns.

But it was the lower panel that held him.

It had been dismissed for years—a decorative addition, a provincial embellishment of Revelation. But Nicodemus had always known better. Now, in the heat and ruin, the truth revealed itself like breath on cold glass.

Four riders. Faint, faded, almost invisible unless the light hit just right.

They emerged from the clouds behind Golgotha, not abstract, but precise. One raised a sword. Another gripped a scale. The third held reins. The last rode without hands, cloaked in shadow.

War. Conquest. Famine. Death.

Not allegory. Not metaphor. Memory.

Their eyes were the worst part. Not fury. Not mercy. Just… recognition. As if they had seen this world burn before. As if they were returning to it.

Beneath them, curling through the dust and gold leaf, the pattern writhed.

Seven arcs. Concentric. Spiralling.

Not a flourish. A seal.

Lapis pigment clung stubbornly to the wall, refusing to burn. It pulsed in the flicker of firelight like something remembered. Like something waiting.

Nicodemus fell to his knees.

He wasn't praying. He was listening.

Outside, the fortress bell fell silent. Cannon fire echoed from the coast. The Ottoman banner had risen over the ridge hours ago. Kolossi would fall by morning.

But here, beneath the fresco, time twisted.

He felt it: this moment had happened before.

Would happen again.

The spiral wasn't prophecy.

It was repetition. And the Horsemen weren't judgment. They were return.

A beam gave way above him. Stone split.

The last thing Father Nicodemus saw was the rider cloaked in ash, turning to face him. Not with rage.

With patience.

Then the vault collapsed.

And the fresco disappeared beneath centuries of silence.

CHAPTER 20

YORKSHIRE – WINTER 1992

The snow came early that year—wet flakes clinging to the old stones of the cottage and dampening the world to silence.

Claire sat by the hearth with a book open across her knees. But she hadn't turned a page in twenty minutes.

William Armitage leaned in the doorway. His cane rested against the wall. He hadn't spoken since breakfast.

'Dad?'

He looked over.

That place in Cyprus,' she said. 'Kolossi. The chapel…'

He waited.

'There was something in that fresco. The halos. The alignment. It wasn't just art. '

William nodded once. 'No. It wasn't. '

She blinked. 'You… knew?'

'I saw things too. Once. ' He crossed the room slowly, lowered himself into the armchair across from her. 'Things I didn't have words for. Still don't. '

She frowned, unsure if he was teasing or warning.

'What kind of things?'

He looked at the fire. Not at her.

'They don't come with names, Clare-bear. They come with weight. They settle into your bones, and one day— years later—you'll realise they've been shaping you the whole time. '

She said nothing.

He reached into his coat and pulled out a worn scrap of paper—creased, folded a dozen times. He handed it to her.

On it was a charcoal sketch: a horse rearing in silhouette, its limbs looping into crescents.

'I found that in the Balkans. Drew it before I even realised I'd seen it. '

Claire traced the lines with her eyes. 'It's like… It's in motion. But not moving. '

'That's the thing,' William said. 'Some memories aren't yours. Doesn't mean they're not true. '

She looked up.

He nodded toward the sketch. 'Keep it. One day you might need to remember something that never happened. '

HEREFORD – WINTER 1995

The house had gone quiet. His daughter had returned to Cambridge. His wife, to the earth.

✳ ✳ ✳

Adam Hayes found the file in a forgotten drawer deep in the Regiment archive—thin, dusty, and stamped:

DECLASSIFIED

The name on the cover stopped him cold:

ARMITAGE, WILLIAM.

UNIT: RED TEAM — SPECIAL OPERATIONS

It wasn't a long file.

Commendations. Citations. A summary of Operation HIGHVALE — sealed for over a decade.

Then a final note: Final engagement resulted in critical injury and unilateral withdrawal from active duty. No formal debrief. Beneath that, a second line:

Status: ***Removed at own request.*** And at the very bottom, scrawled by hand in the margin: ***Chose silence over ceremony.***

Adam stared at the words for a long moment. Then he closed the file, packed a bag, and drove north.

✳ ✳ ✳

YORKSHIRE DALES — TWO DAYS LATER

The cottage sat beneath the ridge, stone walls, slate roof, wind curling across the moor like memory.

William Armitage opened the door without surprise. Older. Lean. Still sharp behind the eyes.

80

He stood on one leg—the other replaced by a carbon-fibre prosthetic visible beneath the cuff of his trousers. A weathered cane leaned against the wall beside him.

'Hayes,' he said.

'Sir. '

They sat by the fire in silence.

No questions. No briefings.

Just whisky and smoke, and the long pause between two men scarred by the same machine.

'You read the file,' Armitage said.

'I did. '

'You come to see if I was dead?'

'No,' Adam said.

'I came to see if I'm becoming you. '

Armitage stared into the fire.

'And?'

'I don't know yet. '

A long silence.

Then Armitage spoke, voice low, words shaped by years of weight: 'You don't win by surviving. You win by not letting them turn your silence into stone. '

Adam stood. Set his glass down.

Didn't salute. Didn't thank him. Just nodded. Then stepped back into the fog, carrying not answers, but the shape of a future carved in silence.

CHAPTER 21
CAMBRIDGE, 1995

The bells rang through the fog like a memory she hadn't asked for.

Claire stood just outside the chapel, her fingers tightening around the strap of her satchel. Inside, the final hymn had started. She could hear it through the thick oak door—something stiff-lipped and well-meaning. The same tune they'd used at the service a week ago.

Her mother's funeral.

Her mum had died quickly. Cancer, they said. A short, brutal sprint through diagnosis and decline. Claire had watched the light leave in flickers—not all at once, but in small, cruel withdrawals: first her appetite, then her hair, then her voice. By the end, her mum just nodded when Claire entered the room. Still smiling. Always smiling.

William had been composed. Courteous. Impeccable. He shook hands with mourners, stood straight at the graveside, and delivered a military courtesy so complete it made Claire feel like an intruder at her own mother's burial. He hadn't cried. Not then. Not in the days after.

But Mrs. Fullerton from next door had told her: he stood alone in the garden that night, unmoving, for nearly an hour.

Claire hadn't known what to do with that.

She stepped into the chapel now, late, letting the music cover her entrance. The walls were ancient stone. The windows filtered watery daylight onto the flagstones. She found a seat near the back.

Dr. Meredith from the Warburg guest program sat two rows ahead. He didn't turn, but she knew he'd clocked her presence. Always did.

After the hymn ended, the lecture began—something on Marian iconography and late Gothic form. Claire took notes, but her hand moved slowly. Her eyes drifted to the stained-glass panel above the pulpit: a crucifixion scene, haloed and rigid.

In the lower corner: three small loops. Stylised. Familiar.

The fleur-de-lis again.

She frowned—then circled the fleur-de-lis in her notes, tracing it once, twice, until the ink bled memory

Later, in the college library, she reopened her Cyprus notebook. Her mother's handwriting was still there on the edge of the page: 'Symmetry in sorrow can be beautiful too. '

Claire traced the words with her thumb. Her mum had said that standing in Kolossi Castle, gazing at the crumbling fresco—Mary and John, Christ above a skull, the fleur-de-lis tucked into the hem of the robe. Back then, Claire thought it was just a flourish.

Now, it was something else.

She pulled her research folder from her satchel and spread sketches across the desk: tracings of crucifixion scenes, notations from medieval altarpieces, floor plans of abbey chapels. The same symbol repeated across five sites. Different regions. Different centuries. Same placement. Same geometry.

She began overlaying them, layering one over another until a pattern began to emerge. Seven arcs. A spiral alignment. Not decoration. Not theology.

A memory. A signal.

Her grief had nowhere else to go, so it went into structure.

* * *

That weekend, she took the early train to London.

The Warburg Institute archive held material Cambridge didn't—sealed reproductions, Vatican correspondences, forgotten marginalia. Dr. Meredith had vouched for her access, but even that had its limits.

In the manuscript reading room, Claire laid her notes out carefully, arranging them around a borrowed facsimile of a Bruges woodcut. The skull at Golgotha was ringed by a spiral of bones—barely visible unless you were looking for it.

She was.

'Miss Armitage. '

She looked up. Dr. Leonard Marsh stood beside an unfamiliar man—tall, grey-haired, dressed in a charcoal coat with fine lapels and watchful eyes.

'This is Dr. Bellini,' Marsh said. 'He's consulting with the Vatican's sacred art division. ' A pause. 'He's asked to see your thesis notes. '

Claire hesitated. 'Of course. '

Bellini offered a thin smile. 'Your interpretations are... imaginative. '

'They're structural,' she replied calmly.

'And perhaps,' he said, 'unwise. '

She blinked. 'How do you mean?'

He stepped closer, eyes scanning her papers.

'You suggest these symbols form a code. A resonance memory mapped through religious art. You imply intent. '

'I don't imply it,' she said. 'The recurrence is too precise. '

Bellini nodded slowly, as if disappointed.

'Some truths are designed for contemplation. Not excavation. Be cautious, Miss Armitage. Curiosity is a virtue until it becomes trespass. '

He let the words hang.

Then, a final glance toward her spiral sketch, and a quiet warning:

'There are many doors in this field. Not all of them open outward. '

He left without looking back.

Claire stood frozen for a moment, then looked down at her notes. One page was missing. Just one.

She exhaled slowly. Reached for her pen. On a clean sheet, she wrote: REPETITION IS NOT A COINCIDENCE. IT'S A CODE. MUM. KOLOSSI. SYMBOLS. CYCLE.

Her hand trembled slightly. Not from fear. From conviction.

Two nights later, the spiral woke her again.

Even in sleep, it circled behind her eyelids—seven arcs winding inward like a maze or a memory she hadn't inherited yet.

Claire sat cross-legged on the floor of her tiny room, a desk lamp casting warm light across the spread of books, sketches, and crumpled notes. Her satchel still lay where she'd dropped it after returning from London. The notebook with the missing page was on top.

She reached for it now, then slowly removed a second item she hadn't told anyone about.

A folded slip of acid-free archival paper, taken from the Warburg manuscript room. It wasn't the original, of course, but a reproduction facsimile of a 1492 Vatican woodcut. One that wasn't meant to be copied, traced, or taken.

Claire had memorised its contours.

She unfolded it now. The image was faint. At first glance, just another Passion scene—Christ on the cross, Mary weeping, John turned sideways in despair.

But in the lower margin, behind the skull at Golgotha, the pattern whispered itself into being: a double spiral, nested in a triangle, encircled by seven marks that looked more astrological than Christian.

She laid it flat, then began to redraw it by hand, line by line, using a 0. 3mm Rotring pen. Every detail was burned into her mind. Not just remembered. Internalised.

'Some truths are designed for contemplation,' Bellini had said. 'Not excavation. '

But truth didn't obey rules. And she was done with permission.

Half an hour passed. Then an hour.

When she finally sat back, the re-creation was complete—black ink on smooth vellum. Her own copy. Her own record.

She clipped it into her notes, adding a title at the top of the page: VATICAN CODE – UNRECORDED ALIGNMENT – POSSIBLY PRE-CYCLICAL

Underneath, she wrote: Do not trust the gaps. Trace them.

She stared at her work. Not with triumph. Not with fear.

With resolve.

They could remove access. They could warn her off. But they couldn't remove the pattern from her mind—or the need to uncover its origin.

This was hers now.

For the first time in a week, she felt something other than ache. It was direction—sharp, electric.

She would find the origin of the pattern. She would trace it through centuries, through ritual, through faith and fire. Not because her mum asked her to.

But because in that final hour, her mum had still believed in meaning. Even as her body gave way, her eyes had sought symmetry in sorrow.

Claire would honour that.

Not with silence. But with discovery.

CHAPTER 22

SARAJEVO, 1994

The old theatre stank of soot, piss, and stale vodka—rot layered over history, like the building had been mourning too long to care.

Viktor Tarlen stepped through the buckled side door, the broken lock still swinging on a rusted hinge. He kicked through a ragged curtain, boots crunching glass, plaster, and something finer—ashes, maybe. Or bone.

'Which one's mine?' he asked.

The fixer—barely twenty, face cratered with old burns—jerked his thumb toward a steel crate half-buried under the collapsed ticket counter.

Tarlen moved slowly. Deliberate. He crouched and brushed soot from the crate's pitted surface. Not Russian. Not NATO. New, clean steel—but without a country. A weapon with no flag, no origin.

A mark was etched into the side, almost erased by heat: a horse's hind leg, the curl of a flame, a spiral of motion turning inward. The rest was slagged off by fire—but the shape still pulsed beneath the grime.

Not a brand. Not a warning. A scar.

He paused. Not from curiosity. Instinct. The kind that makes wolves freeze mid-stride when something ancient brushes past.

The fixer shifted. 'Shipment's bound for Belfast. Routed through Vienna, then Limerick. Broker's name was... Vega, maybe? It's all smoke and mirrors. Quiet money. Not cartel. Not political. '

Tarlen didn't reply. But his fingers lingered too long on the melted glyph.

There was something about it—not remembered in thought, but in blood. In pressure behind the eyes. A rhythm that matched his pulse.

He closed the lid. Lit a cigarette from his jacket. Didn't look back.

'Send it,' he said. Then vanished into the smoke—like something the war had remembered.

✳ ✳ ✳

LAGOS, 1997

The symbol appeared again—this time on the underside of a biometric case smuggled into the delta during a fuel strike. Tarlen found it while checking the seals.

Same strokes. Same horse. Same faint scorch ring around the flame.

No one else noticed. But Tarlen did.

He wiped the mark clean, then covered it again with dust. Didn't ask questions. Just noted the coincidence.

Six weeks later, the compound burned to the foundations during a blackout firefight. Seventeen bodies. No clear cause.

The pattern continued.

MYANMAR, 2001

A burnt village in Shan State. Civilians. Rebels. No one knew who struck first.

Tarlen arrived late—contracted to protect an opium corridor, but in truth just cleaning up loose ends. In the debris of a collapsed hut, he found a shell casing— standard NATO design but custom-inscribed.

Same symbol. Same damned horse.

No crate this time. Just ash.

He didn't tell anyone.

Didn't keep the casing either.

He just stood there a little longer than usual.

And left.

***

Tarlen never believed in signs. He believed in leverage, in force, in the mathematics of fear. But the mark followed him—Sarajevo, Lagos, Myanmar, and beyond.

Wherever it appeared, something burned.

Governments fell. Orders collapsed. Men disappeared.

He always assumed it belonged to someone else—some silent network, some buried order. What he never considered… was that it marked him.

He didn't know what it meant. But the symbol always came first. And then the fire followed.

CHAPTER 23

LONDON, 1998

Claire stood at the attic window of her flat, the morning light slicing through a crack in the blind, turning dust into golden threads. Boxes sat half-packed on the floor behind her. The flat was being emptied of books, not memories.

She ran her thumb along the edge of an old folder—Cambridge notes, barely touched since she left. There was the sketch of the fresco at Kolossi Castle. The spiral etched into the sky behind the crucified Christ. A crown of arcs. Seven.

That fresco had followed her. Not in the literal sense, but it had shaped her. Cyprus was where the silence began. Cambridge had only magnified it. And her research since had almost consumed it.

Bellini had warned her. That truth burned like a phosphorus flare in her mind even now. 'Some patterns are too big for a single life to hold,' he had said. 'Some cycles devour their observers. '

She hadn't answered him. She still didn't know how.

Claire opened a slim envelope tucked into the back of the folder. Her father's handwriting, weathered by time. Not a confession. Not quite a farewell. Just a fragment:

_'You asked me once what I saw in that chapel. I saw what I wasn't supposed to. Not prophecy. Not madness. Just a wound in time. You're old enough now to follow it.

But remember this: some knowledge resists ownership. It owns you instead.

Love always, W. A. '

She folded it slowly, deliberately, and placed it inside the notebook she was taking to Washington. It wasn't a permanent post, but the Smithsonian had invited her to continue her work in Washington—initially short-term, now open-ended. They'd shown interest in her thesis on apocalyptic iconography and resonance motifs. Enough to bring her over.

But she had questions. And someone at the Smithsonian had finally agreed to listen.

Claire turned from the window, leaving the spiral and the light behind her. For now.

CHAPTER 24
HEREFORD — 1997

The rain in Hereford never asked questions. It just came—slow and grey, soaking parade ground cracks and hissing off slate rooftops like it had nowhere better to be.

Inside the regimental war room, the map was already pinned to the board—Central America, ink still wet at the edges, bleeding into the soft grain of the paper.

Adam stood near the wall, arms crossed, silent.

Tony slouched in the second chair, boots on the table's edge—until Ellis's glare made them drop with a thud.

He reached for the enamel mug he'd smuggled in, took a long sip of what he proudly called 'standard NATO brew. '

'What's in it?' Ellis asked, not really wanting to know.

'Jet fuel, instant granules, and regret,' Tony said. 'Just like Bastion. Keeps the nightmares and the bowel movements on time. '

'Belize,' Ellis said, tapping the map with a blunt finger. 'Joint op. You'll rotate through the British Army Training Support Unit. Officially, it's capacity-building. Unofficially—liaison with a cross-agency task force targeting narco-trafficking routes. '

Tony raised an eyebrow. 'We training jungle commandos or babysitting border guards?'

'Bit of both,' Ellis replied. 'The government's getting squeezed—north by the cartels, south by corruption. You'll embed with a Belizean interdiction unit. Their lead contact is ex-Coast Guard. Callsign: Jaguar. '

Adam nodded. 'Cartel links?'

Ellis's mouth tightened. 'Running guns, coke, people. Honduras through Guatemala into the Caribbean. Someone's equipping them with NATO-grade kit—night vision, comms, surplus tech they shouldn't have. '

He handed over a battered dossier. 'It's not just cartel movement anymore,' he said. 'Two weeks ago, a jungle patrol went dark near the border. NEXA chalked it up to terrain. We're not so sure. '

He lowered his voice. 'Some of the packets we intercepted—they're not cartel. Too clean. Too structured. They're not encrypted the way human comms are. MI6 flagged them as part of a prototype system. Machine learning. Possibly self-adaptive. '

Tony snorted. 'You mean AI?

Ellis didn't smile. 'Call it what you like. It's calculating something. Repeating it. Not random. '

Adam frowned. 'Where's it coming from?'

Ellis slid a blurred satellite schematic from the folder. 'Low orbit. Signals are bouncing through a comms window linked to something called Helion. No official record. No registered project. But it's transmitting. And it's watching. '

He tapped the map again. 'Whatever this is, it's not just human intel. Someone's running simulations. And they're targeting the storm corridor. '

Tony gave a low whistle. 'Merry bloody Christmas. '

The door opened.

A civilian stepped in—a linen shirt under a navy blazer, hair too neat for Hereford, and the wrong kind of polish.

'This is Mr. Keane,' Ellis said. 'Foreign Office liaison. '

Keane's smile was brief, bloodless. 'You'll go in under light cover. Contractors. Jungle specialists. If you're compromised, the line goes dead. Understood?'

Tony muttered, 'Always comforting. '

'One name's surfaced,' Keane added. "Sombra. ' Spanish for shadow. Could be cartel. Could be something else. We want eyes on it. '

* * *

Half a world away, Solis closed a logistics report and stared at the embossed seal on the final page.

A rearing horse. Spiralled beneath it like a wave or a storm. Third time this month.

He told himself it was a coincidence. But deep down, he knew better. It wasn't coincidence.

It was recurrence.

* * *

Back in the war room, Adam didn't blink. 'Rules of engagement?'

'Minimal,' Keane said. 'But be smart. The Americans are sniffing around. The last thing we need is a blue-on-blue with some DEA cowboy who thinks he's in a Tom Clancy novel. '

Ellis passed two sealed envelopes across the table. 'Passports. Contacts. Sat-freqs. You deploy in forty-eight. Pack for wet, hot, and hostile. '

Tony grinned. 'Jungle it is. So much for downtime. '

Adam's eyes drifted back to the map. The Belize River coiled like a green snake through jungle thick with red-marked sectors: No Contact.

Something about the mission scratched at the back of his mind—not the danger. That was familiar. It was the gaps. The pieces left unsaid.

He looked up. 'Any chance this turns political?'

Ellis gave a thin smile. 'Adam, everything turns political. Especially when it starts in the jungle. '

As Ellis gathered the documents, one folder slipped from the stack. Just a flash—but Adam caught it.

A dark seal, pressed into parchment-hued paper. Four strokes. A rearing horse framed by a spiral.

No one else seemed to notice.

But Adam filed it away.

A symbol doesn't appear by accident.

CHAPTER 25
BELIZE 1997

Inside, the safe house was hot and still. Books were stacked like barricades—climate science, field manuals, dog-eared intelligence reports. A shortwave receiver buzzed softly on the shelf.

Rosa crossed the room, pulled a battered recorder from the rack, and pressed play.

A burst of static filled the space. Then—faint, clipped tones. A tight burst of sound like code buried in rain. Then silence. A pause. The pattern repeated.

'We picked that up yesterday,' she said. 'Not cartel. Not weather. Ran it through everything—came back clean. But it loops. Every ninety-one minutes. '

Adam stepped closer, frowning. 'Low orbit cycle?'

'Or someone pretending to be. '

Tony leaned back against the wall, arms crossed. 'This kind of chatter used to drive a CIA guy I knew mad. Ross. Analyst out of D. C. —obsessed with patterns no one else noticed. '

Adam glanced at him. 'You worked with him?'

'Not officially,' Tony said. 'But he owed me a favour after Kosovo. Smart bastard. The kind who connected dots before they even appeared. '

Rosa moved to the centre table, unrolling a battered topographic map. The surface was stained and torn, its corners curled from years of use. She pointed with a pen to a bend in the river.

'That signal's bouncing from here. Just past an old supply trail. '

Tony traced the river line with a knuckle. 'And the last patrol?'

'Six men. No contact for two days. '

She hesitated, then added, quieter, 'My brother died in that stretch. Three years ago. '

Tony looked up.

'We called it a flood,' she said. 'That's what went in the report. The easy version. '

She moved to a drawer, pulled out a faded photo, and laid it on the table. Six Belizean soldiers—sunlit, squinting, alive. One of them, younger, bore her face in the eyes. In the corner, etched faintly into a crate behind them, was a symbol—weathered, precise. A horse.

Her hand lingered on the edge of the photo just a moment too long. Then she let go.

'I saw that mark again last month. A courier manifest, pulled from a crash. Same ink. Same style. But the paper —aged. Like it had waited somewhere dry enough to forget time. '

Adam stared at the image. The symbol caught him in the chest like a punch.

He'd seen it before—buried in a sealed file marked for destruction. He hadn't opened it. He hadn't needed to. The seal was enough.

Tony leaned closer. 'You said your brother's team disappeared. '

'They didn't vanish,' Rosa said. 'They burned. '

Her voice was steady. Too steady.

'No blast. No shrapnel. No chemical trace. Just… heat. The boots melted. No bones. No sound. Just the quiet, and shadows burnt into the ground. '

The silence settled in around them—thick, aware.

'I reported it. The Americans blamed cartel interference. My agency chalked it up to jungle ghosts. But I was there. Three days after. '

She looked straight at Adam.

'It was wrong. The air was too still. No birds. No insects. The trees didn't move. It felt like the earth forgot how to breathe. '

Tony exhaled slowly. 'You think 'Sombra' is more than a name. '

'I think it's a signal,' she said. 'A beginning. And I think someone's been trying to finish what they started long before we were born. '

She turned the map over. Burned into the underside, barely visible beneath the dust, was the same horse symbol—hidden, deliberate.

Tony raised an eyebrow. 'Bit early in the trip for ghosts. '

Adam didn't answer.

He'd stopped believing in coincidence a long time ago.

✷ ✷ ✷

At 0400, Rosa knocked once. Sharp. No hesitation. 'You're up. We've got movement near the signal origin. '

Tony sat up, rubbing his face. 'No coffee?'

'You'll be sweating it out by sunrise. Move. '

They geared up without a word. Weapons checked. Packs light. Machetes oiled.

Outside, the jungle loomed—dense and dark, thick with breath.

They stepped into it.

Adam took point. Tony watched their six. Rosa guided them, machete flashing in silence.

After twenty minutes, the safe house vanished behind them.

'Jaguar's unit was supposed to meet us at the ridge,' Rosa muttered, almost like a confession. 'They pulled out two days ago. No word. No reason. Just gone. '

Adam didn't look back. He felt it in his chest—tight, cold.

This wasn't just another mission.

This was someone else's ground.

* * *

She'd doubled back while the others pushed toward the ridge.

The air was heavier now. Still. She stood by the receiver, eyes fixed on the topographic map.

Her notes were still spread across the table — signal loops, satellite overlays, the old photo, the torn page with the spiral codes she hadn't explained.

She stared at them for a long time. Then she moved.

Folded each item with care. Slipped them into a battered folder. Added a printout of the last transmission spike.

She hesitated. Then took a pen and wrote one name on the front in clean, block capitals:

ROSS

She knelt beside the shortwave cabinet, pulled up a loose floorboard, and slid the folder beneath. Not out of fear. Out of instinct. They were close. But not ready. Not yet.

Then she stood, turned out the light, and followed the path into the trees.

She didn't see the shape waiting beyond the ridge.

CHAPTER 26

The river moved slowly that day, sluggish and brown, choked with silt from an early storm. Rosa Calderón sat on the bow of the patrol boat, boots kicked up, her clipboard catching drops of sweat instead of ink.

Her brother, Javier, stood behind the tiller. Tall. Broad. The kind of man who made others feel steady just by breathing beside them.

He grinned. 'You're not built for this heat, Hermana. '

She tossed a mango pit into the water. 'I'm built for truth, not mosquitoes. '

Javier laughed. 'Truth doesn't mean much if you forget how to feel it. This place talks. You just have to listen. '

Rosa rolled her eyes. 'The jungle doesn't talk, Javi. It steams, it bites, and it rots your boots. '

He pointed upriver. 'There. You hear that?'

Birdsong. Distant howler monkeys. A low, humming static of insect life.

'It's normal,' she said.

'It's loud,' he corrected. 'Because when it goes quiet, that's when we worry. '

She didn't respond. Instead, she scribbled a note about water levels—already higher than forecast—and switched the channel on the radio. Static. Then, a faint click. A signal looped on repeat—unlabeled, encrypted, too short to make sense.

'Getting that again,' she said. 'The weird pulse. '

Javier's smile faded. 'That's been bouncing for weeks. '

She frowned. 'Command says it's spillover from a DEA op. '

His grip tightened on the tiller. 'Command says a lot. '

They rounded a bend where the trees leaned lower like they were eavesdropping. A faint breeze stirred. It smelled wrong—like burned iron.

Rosa's eyes narrowed. 'Javi, do you—'

Then the boat rocked.

Something large moved beneath them—just a ripple, too big for fish, too slow for current. The engine stuttered.

Rosa looked up. The canopy was still.

Silent.

Javier's voice dropped. 'Back downstream. Now. '

She didn't argue.

As he turned them around, she caught a glimpse of something on the riverbank—a crate. Partially buried, marked with a faint, weatherworn sigil—a horse rearing inside a spiral.

She didn't know what it meant. Not yet.

CHAPTER 27

BELIZE JUNGLE — AUGUST 1997

The jungle steamed. A low, animal breath rising from the trees, from the wet earth, from the power cables strung too low through the mud. Sofia Castellano moved between the tents like smoke. The guards knew her, barely nodded. One of them—Perdomo, always chewing on a cinnamon stick—reached out to tousle her hair. She ducked him without a word.

She wasn't supposed to be here.

For most of her life, Sofia had lived far from her father's world—in stone halls and manicured gardens, surrounded by Latin textbooks and boarding school bells. A private education. All expenses paid. But no birthday calls. No visits. Just tuition invoices marked 'cleared. '

When her mother died that spring—Panama City, pneumonia, a quiet room with no priest—Sofia had expected silence from him too. Instead, she got a letter.

He wanted her to come.

Not forever. Just for the summer.

To reconnect. To talk. To begin again.

And for a while, she let herself believe it.

He had been kind, even warm, in those first few days. Strange, but careful. He showed her the compound, the generators, the way the jungle curved when the rains were late. He called her by her name—not mi hija, not child, but Sofia—like he was trying to say it right again.

She wanted to trust him.

But now it had been three days without a word. No explanation. No summons. No glance from across the planning table. She asked one of the aides. He said her father was 'occupied. '

Something was wrong. Or something was happening.

Sofia slipped past the satellite trucks, past the humming rows of generators and their diesel stink. She kept to the edges of the paths. The air here didn't feel right. It was too hot for the hour. Too still.

She found the crates first.

Stacked behind a camouflaged tarp, half-sunken in mud, stamped with aid insignias from half a dozen agencies. USAID. Red Crescent. The spiral mark her father had told her never to draw.

She crouched beside one, peeled the tarp. The topmost crate was labelled 'MEDICAL – MALARIA. ' She opened it.

Empty.

Her breath caught. She tried another. And another. The same.

Then she heard the whine.

A thin electric drone coming from deeper in the tree line. Not a generator. Not a vehicle. Something worse.

She crept closer. Past the crates. Past the perimeter posts. She knew how to move. Her father had taught her. She knew how to find the weak spaces in a fence. How to stay invisible.

She reached a clearing. The grass was burned into perfect rings.

A dish—no, an antenna, but coiled like a serpent—was humming on a raised gantry, pointed at the clouds. No one stood near it. But cables led away into the forest, to something she couldn't see.

Her throat tightened. She didn't know what it was. Only that it shouldn't be here.

She whispered to no one, or maybe to the trees:

'You said this would make things better. '

Sofia turned. She didn't remember walking back to the camp. Her hands were shaking. Her skin itched like she'd stood too long near something that hated her.

She reached into her pocket.

The bracelet was still there. Copper, scratched, threaded with green and ochre beads—too small now.

Javier had given it to her three nights ago, just before the rains started. He was young, soft-voiced, and stationed at the outer generator bank—a junior technician, or so she'd been told.

He had been kind. Asked questions no one else did. Laughed too easily. Sat beside her at meals when others avoided eye contact.

Her father had noticed. Solis had frowned, said nothing at first—but the message was clear. Sofia was sixteen. Javier was a stranger. Unvetted. A face that wouldn't stay around for long. Her father would see to that.

But before he disappeared, Javier had pressed the bracelet into her palm.

'Names matter,' he said. 'Sometimes people forget what they are to the world. This helps them remember. '

He didn't explain what it meant.

She didn't ask.

She sat by the water tanks. She could still hear the hum in her ears.

Two of the technicians walked past. She didn't know their names. One of them said something about Javier. Said the test had been successful. That the frequencies lined up. That the field had held.

'No one told the locals to evacuate?'

The other man shrugged. 'Didn't matter. Command cleared it. '

She didn't cry. She just sat there, gripping the bracelet, pressing it into her palm until it left a mark.

That night, her father walked with her beyond the compound. Toward the ruins.

They didn't speak, but she felt it—that they were being watched. Not by the usual patrols or command staff. Something colder. Older. Like the jungle itself had turned to look.

At one point, her father paused, eyes sweeping the treeline. His voice was almost a whisper.

'Keep walking. '

She looked up at him. His expression told her what he didn't say:

He felt it too.

She didn't reach for his hand.

She didn't ask questions.

She just walked. The distance between them had already begun.

There were no explanations. Only the weight of knowing too little, and the quiet certainty that something had changed.

That night, the jungle shook again.

Sofia didn't wake.

She was already standing. Eyes open, staring out into the dark, clutching the bracelet. She would keep it. She didn't know why it mattered to her.

Perhaps just that Javier had been kind. Showed an interest.

CHAPTER 28
SIX WEEKS BEFORE THE FLOOD – CENTRAL BELIZE

The jungle was unnaturally still.

Sergeant Javier Calderón swept his rifle left, then right, as his patrol advanced through dense underbrush. Five soldiers moved with him in staggered formation— silent, alert. The heat was oppressive, but the sweat didn't unsettle him.

It was the absence.

No insects. No birds. No wind.

'Something's wrong,' Larios muttered behind him.

Javier raised a clenched fist. The unit halted.

They had been sent to investigate an unexplained thermal anomaly—classified as a 'resonance spike' by Nexa Systems. No real explanation. Just coordinates, a last-minute reroute, and a quiet warning from Rosa the night before: 'Watch the patterns. If it feels wrong, it is. '

It felt wrong.

The trees opened into a clearing—unnaturally round, as if carved by design. A tall, blackened apparatus stood at the centre on a scorched metal tripod, humming faintly. Smaller pylons ringed it like stakes driven into the soil. The ground here was dry—too dry. Steam lifted in slow, spiralling coils.

'What the hell is that?' Larios asked.

The radio static hissed louder. No signal in or out.

Ten kilometres away, inside a Nexa mobile command unit, a technician leaned forward.

'New telemetry spike. Thermal flare trending upward. We've got movement—six warm bodies. '

Solis stood behind him, arms folded. 'Overlay the location. '

The map flickered—dense jungle, overlaid with pulsing thermographic contours. At the centre: a perfect circle, glowing faintly.

'What's that clearing?'

'No designation, sir. But something's been transmitting from there on and off for days. '

Solis didn't answer. He just watched.

✳ ✳ ✳

Javier stepped closer. The air vibrated subtly, like standing too close to a power station. He crouched beside the main device. Strange, worn symbols were etched into its casing. One caught his eye: a galloping horse, or what was left of it—its shape collapsing into spirals, as though burned and re-etched a dozen times. It looked like something remembered wrong, as if even the metal had forgotten what it once meant.

He'd seen that symbol before.

Three weeks ago, he'd spent just five days posing as a junior technician in Solis's outer camp—installing cable, pretending not to understand the systems around him. His orders were to observe, map Nexa's layout, and confirm whether the rumours about tests were true.

That's where he'd seen her.

Sofia.

No older than sixteen. Pale, distant eyes ringed with grief. She passed him once by the auxiliary tents, carrying a thick notebook, her face turned inward. He later heard her mother had died.

He hadn't meant to speak. But something about her silence—how it wrapped around her like armour—stirred something human.

He slipped the bracelet from his wrist. A loop of thread and green-and-ochre beads. Around a copper band. Simple. Worn. Just like the one he'd given his sister before her first northern patrol.

Sofia hadn't replied. She'd looked at him for a long moment and nodded.

Then she was gone.

He hadn't expected to see her again.

He reached for his radio.

Static.

'All units, fall back,' Javier said. 'This isn't secure—'

The air snapped.

A low-frequency vibration pulsed outward from the device. The clearing trembled. Trees leaned inward. One soldier dropped screaming. Another clutched his chest and staggered into the brush.

'Move!' Javier shouted. 'Now!'

The pulse hit again—deeper, sharper. Larios vanished mid-step. No flash. No flame. Just a shimmer—and he was gone.

Javier turned to signal retreat, but the heat struck like a wave, blurring his vision. The machine pulsed a third time. Leaves curled inward. The jungle blackened without burning.

He staggered back. His ears rang.

The bracelet. He'd given it to her for a reason—proof, identity, maybe even protection. Now it would have to do.

He fumbled for his notebook, tearing the flap open, pen jerking across the page.

Two words. ***They return.***

And then—white.

✳ ✳ ✳

Back in the Nexa command unit, the telemetry spiked. Field collapse,' the technician muttered. 'All six life signs —lost. '

Solis said nothing. Just six blinking points on a screen —gone.

The encrypted line buzzed.

'The curve held,' said Vega. His voice was steady, unhurried. 'Septem thresholds confirmed. The seventh vector finally stabilised. '

Solis narrowed his eyes. 'You didn't mention we had boots on the ground. '

'It wasn't relevant to Helion's test,' Vega replied. 'The system needed resonance feedback. It needed to feel the break. '

'They were soldiers,' Solis said coldly. 'Not noise. '

'They were within Septem's arc. The seals open either way.

''They mattered. ''The pattern doesn't care. '

The line cut.

Solis stood slowly, hands behind his back, watching the screen flicker to static.

Shut it down. Wipe the logs. Transfer the raw data to my private server. '

'You want it classified?'

Solis shook his head. 'No,' he said. 'I want it forgotten.
'

✳ ✳ ✳

Three days later, the search teams found nothing. No bodies. No crater. No traces of a blast. Just fused earth—smooth as glass—and a single corrupted drone frame: six figures entering the clearing. The next frame was white.
There were no names. No faces. No trail.

✳ ✳ ✳

Rosa never saw what happened. She never needed to.

Weeks later, scanning satellite stills from Nexa's support camps, she paused on one frame. A girl standing near a cargo crate. Pale. Downcast. Alone.

On her wrist: a woven bracelet—green and ochre thread.

Javier had given it to Sofia.

A kindness.

A mark of hope.

A way to know who she was—if the world ever looked for her.

They hadn't vanished. They had been erased.

CHAPTER 29
PRAGUE, CZECH REPUBLIC – 2003

The bar smelled of wet ash and lemon oil. Thorne swirled his drink, a finger of whisky neat, with a plastic cocktail sword shaped like a crucifix. The irony was not lost on him.

A young man sat across from him, sweat at his collar, the look of someone freshly inducted into a world he didn't understand.

'Are you certain this footage will hold?' the young man asked. 'The village wasn't even in the province. '

Thorne smiled faintly. 'It doesn't matter. It will resonate. '

'But when they check—'

'They won't. Because by then, the question won't be whether it happened. It'll be whether it might happen again. Fear doesn't wait for proof. '

He finished his drink and slid a manila envelope across the table. Inside were photographs—bodies staged in positions to mimic a massacre.

The television in the corner bar shifted. Emergency elections. Collapse of a coalition.

'The Prime Minister has resigned,' the barkeep said in Czech.

Thorne stood. 'Truth,' he murmured, 'is a currency. I prefer futures. '

He left the bar. In the folder he left behind, a symbol was stamped on the last page: a stylised scale, its pans tipped unevenly, with ash spilling from the heavier side.

* * *

GENEVA, SWITZERLAND – PRESENT DAY

The sky was knife-grey over Lake Geneva, the water like slate. Viktor Tarlen didn't look at it. He looked only at the projections on the wall—storm forecasts, migration stress maps, energy grids buckling under theoretical strain.

Behind him, the conference room buzzed with tension. A dozen executives, all mid-level heads from competitor firms, gathered in a forced 'strategic alliance'.

'This isn't a negotiation,' one of them said. 'You don't get to dictate the terms of a global weather modelling protocol. '

Tarlen tapped a button. A hologram of South Sudan appeared—current drought zone in red, next year's projected conflict map in shifting amber.

'I don't dictate,' he said. 'I leverage. '

'You're hijacking the climate for profit. '

'Profit is the veil. Power is the substance. '

Another man stood. 'You kill a harvest, Viktor, you kill thousands. '

Tarlen didn't speak. He simply raised one hand, palm open, then slowly turned it over.

Outside, on the street below, a black sedan exploded.

The tremor in the windows was soft but unmistakable.

Silence followed.

Tarlen turned back to the projections.

'Begin the resonance dampening trials. Route excess data to Helion-9. War begins with harvest. '

'Each node pulls from Septem. Seven harmonic thresholds mapped across stress basins. 'Tarlen's gaze flicked to the rainfall simulation. 'The math doesn't lie. Only people do. '

CHAPTER 30

The flood came faster than the forecasts.

Solis stood ankle-deep in muddy water, watching a Nexa supply truck tilt on its side into a flooded ditch, wheels still spinning as its rear axle disappeared beneath the runoff. The jungle road had become a river overnight. Torrents of brown water surged around his boots, carrying broken branches and fragments of packing crates downstream.

The dam held. That wasn't the failure. The plan was.

He had spent weeks preparing the logistics—vetting contractor security, designing staggered convoy routes, smoothing over border clearances with bribes and memorandums. Every angle accounted for. Every potential delay mapped. But this was the third breakdown in a month.

Not sabotage. Not human error. Just… interruption. Patterned. Predictable. Inexplicable.

He'd seen plenty of operational failure in his career— bad orders, bad intel, bad people. But this felt different. Not a mistake. Not chaos. More like resistance.

A shout cut through the noise of the rushing water. Solis turned.

A local elder approached, moving steadily through the current, barefoot and hunched with age. His robe was soaked to the knee, his grey hair stuck to his scalp. He didn't speak at first—just extended a folded parchment, old and curled at the edges, ink faded nearly to sepia.

Solis took it carefully, shielding it under his jacket. When he opened it, the paper felt soft and damp between his fingers. Drawn in thick, confident strokes were spirals. Coils. Notations that, at first glance, resembled economic flow maps. But the lines didn't reference any known system. No legends. No units. Just motion—organic and deliberate.

He frowned. 'What is this?'

The old man stared past him. 'Not future. Not past. Just motion,' he said. 'You try to fix the wave. We ride it. '

Solis said nothing. The man turned and walked away, leaving wet footprints behind.

***

Back at the Nexa outpost, the air buzzed with the static of overloaded comms and the stench of mildew. Solis sat at his laptop, hunched over rows of convoy logs and satellite overlays. He pulled up movement records from the last three weeks—convoy deviations, route closures, and checkpoint failures.

None of it made sense. No orders had been issued to reroute the trucks, and yet the choke points had collapsed days before the rain. Paths had shifted with perfect timing as if responding to something invisible. He traced the detours on a blank map. One by one, they curved around impassable terrain not yet known to be impassable.

He leaned back, rubbing his temples. Then, he overlaid the parchment.

The match wasn't exact, but it was close enough to make him sit up.

The paths formed a shape. Not a mess. Not a scatter pattern.

A spiral.

He stared at it—a coil. The detours didn't form a failure—they followed a path, not through intention but through design.

But whose?

The engineer in him rejected the idea outright. No model accounted for this kind of predictive disruption unless someone had built one. But even that was conjecture—no evidence—just instinct.

He didn't believe in fate. Never had.

But something was folding around his work, changing the terrain just before he arrived, curving the edges of his precision.

And for the first time in his career, he stopped correcting people who did believe.

CHAPTER 31

BARCELONA, 1992

The wind was rising across the Barcelona hills, a cold breath that whispered through the pine trees and rattled the storm shutters on the Vega estate. Inside, in the shadowed silence of his private study, Hendrik Vega sat alone at his desk, hands resting on a velvet-lined case older than the room itself.

He had retrieved it under false pretences—borrowed, he told the archivist, for 'comparative ecclesiastical study. ' The Vatican would not ask questions. Not of him.

Not yet.

With a slow breath, he opened the clasp and lifted the manuscript free.

Visions of the Stars.

The codex exhaled with age. The leather binding cracked softly. Vellum pages rippled with the dryness of centuries. Even the ink—black, brown, and crimson— seemed alive in the low lamplight. He had studied it before, cautiously, in fragments. But not like this.

Tonight, he would read without flinching.

He turned the first page. And fell into the silence of the stars.

The early folios were maps—celestial renderings etched with obsessive care. Spirals nested within spirals. Planetary orbits overlaid with strange mathematical sequences—not coordinates, but ratios. Harmonic intervals. Familiar, yet impossibly precise.

He reached for a notepad, jotting rapidly. The same values he had once identified, years ago, buried in his early climate-modelling white papers. Abstract ideas. Proofs and conjectures. Never tested.

The manuscript's margins were filled with symbols—sigils Vega hadn't deciphered until years later. Each matched a harmonic event. Not just weather. Not just orbital resonance. Seven breaks. Seven phases. A pattern buried in time itself.

Hendrik hadn't called it by name back then.

Silas had. *Septem.*

He had theorised that planetary resonance could influence Earth's upper atmosphere and that energy might be drawn, shaped, and redirected. But even then, he had warned of limits and consequences. He never intended for it to become a system.

Silas had made it one.

Stellarion. The satellite array. The signal grid. Phase Zero.

Built from fragments. From whispers. From memory, Hendrik hadn't realised he had passed from father to son.

Later pages shifted in tone. Diagrams gave way to anatomical illustrations—bone structures and gene helices interwoven with astrological marks. There was a convergence of blood and orbit, four bloodlines, and four lineages.

Each was marked not by name, but by glyph—one bore a familiar curve, once a horse, now distorted into a vortex. The symbol had changed over the centuries. Where once there was a beast, now there was motion.

He didn't need names. He recognised them in silhouette, in posture. Archetypes, yes—but disturbingly close to the real.

One sketch bore a resemblance to his own son— shoulders hunched in thought, eyes alight with inner storms.

Hendrik remembered the day Silas had seen these years ago when the case had been unguarded. The boy had gone silent. Not out of fear—but wonder—the kind Hendrik hadn't known how to answer.

What had he taken from it?

What had it awakened?

Beneath one of the diagrams, a line was written in cramped red ink:

'They do not inherit power. They inherit memory. '

The thought repelled him.

Not chosen by fate. Bred for recurrence.

Near the end of the codex, a set of schematics emerged —shapes reminiscent of resonance grids and thermal vectors. Their function wasn't immediately apparent. But the patterns pulsed in sync with orbital trajectories on the earlier pages.

He saw echoes of the same waveform models he had once proposed in academic journals—never published. Too speculative. Too dangerous.

He had buried that work years ago.

Not just because it frightened him. But because no one else had.

The universities dismissed it. The ministry shelved it.

And deep down, he had hoped the silence meant it would die there—unnoticed, unproven, forgotten.

But Silas had exhumed it.

Taken it further. Refined the equations. Built the platform. Deployed the satellites. Not because he understood everything, but because something inside him remembered.

My son is already building it, Hendrik thought with a shiver. Not out of malice, but driven by something more profound, an inherited instinct—echoes of a memory he never lived. That terrified Hendrik more than the manuscript itself.

The last page was brittle. Darkened by time. A circular pattern filled the folio, orbit paths folding inward until they vanished into a blackened core. Around its edge, only three words remained legible:

Quattuor. Septem. Iterum - *Four. Seven. Again.*

He closed the book slowly, reverently. He didn't fully understand it. Not yet. But he knew enough to feel the warning in his bones. This was not just history. It was recurrence. And Silas, brilliant and driven, already stood too close to the edge.

He returned the manuscript to its case, sealed it, and placed it deep into the vault. As the locking mechanism hummed to life, Hendrik laid one palm flat against the steel. Not to protect the world from the manuscript. But to protect his son from himself.

'Not yet,' he whispered. 'Not you. Not if I can stop it. '

And the wind rose again beyond the glass, like the sound of distant waves returning to a shore long forgotten.

CHAPTER 32
BELIZEAN JUNGLE 1997

The jungle pressed close, hot, wet, and alive with noise.

But something else stirred beneath the insect hum and the shriek of distant birds.

A tension.

Wrongness.

It crawled beneath the skin like heat behind the eyes.

Adam led, machete low, eyes constantly scanning. Tony moved behind him, lighter on his feet than he looked, checking their six every few paces. Neither spoke. The canopy was too dense for satellite coverage, the undergrowth too tangled for drones. This was boots-on-ground recon—the kind where a mistake didn't earn you a slap on the wrist. It earned you a bullet in the throat.

They'd been moving since before first light, hugging the river until it forked into a feeder stream choked with vines and overhang. Somewhere beyond the bend was the site Rosa had flagged—a suspected drop point. No official intel. Just movement, whispers, and radio ghosts. Enough to check out.

Rosa had split off at dawn to prep the extraction point further north. If things went smooth, they'd rendezvous by nightfall.

Adam raised a fist—halt.

He dropped to one knee and brought his field binoculars to his eyes. Through a break in the foliage, a clearing came into view.

Cargo crates. Steel. Weatherproofed, stacked beneath camo netting.

A hacked-out landing zone—machetes and machines had torn it from the jungle.

Two helicopters sat at the centre. Civilian paint jobs. Too clean. Too new.

Cartel men moved between the crates. Armed. Loose, but not lazy. They knew their trade.

But Adam's eyes tracked past them.

Another group. Cleaner gear. Coordinated. Tactical harnesses. No cartel tattoos. No government insignia.

Mercs.

At the centre of the operation stood a man who didn't need a weapon to command space.

Mid-forties. Weathered. Charisma like oil slick over concrete. He wore desert boots and a pale shirt rolled to the elbows, revealing a faded military tattoo—South American special forces, maybe.

Solis.

A hard case beside him was cracked open—sleek rifles inside. Not junk. Not surplus. Factory new.

Tony crouched beside Adam, silent. He unzipped a side pouch and pulled out the broken-down scope of a suppressed M82. With practised ease, he assembled it—not to shoot, but to see.

Through the magnified lens, he became still.

Breath measured. Focus absolute.

'Three-forty to the crates,' he muttered. 'Wind's clean. That one by the fuel drum—he blinks just before he shifts weight. He's the anchor. '

Adam said nothing. Just listened.

Tony adjusted the dial two clicks left. Paused. Exhaled slowly.

'Could drop five before the sixth hears a thing. '

No pride. No ego. Just fact.

Then, he collapsed the scope and stowed it away.

'But not today. '

Adam gave the slightest nod. Professional. Disciplined. Dangerous.

Then his eyes caught on something else.

A figure behind Solis.

A girl.

Sixteen, maybe. Olive skin. Long braid. A faded baseball cap and a tactical vest too large for her frame. No weapon. No words. Just stillness.

Watching.

She didn't flinch when a man barked orders beside her. Didn't blink at the whine of rotor blades.

Tony's voice dropped. 'His daughter?'

Adam studied her. 'Maybe. Or leverage. '

They stayed low. Watched.

Tony adjusted his focus, narrowing in on her hands.

'That bracelet,' he muttered. 'Copper. Worn flat at the edges. Rosa wears one just like it. '

Adam frowned. 'Could be a coincidence. '

Tony didn't answer. But the look in his eyes said it wasn't.

The girl hadn't moved. She didn't look scared. She looked… aware.

Adam's gaze lingered on the crates, the gear, the silence.

'All this kit. All this surveillance. And we still don't know who we're really fighting. '

He said it quietly, not expecting an answer.

Tony cut him a glance. 'You're starting to ask the wrong kind of questions, mate. '

Adam didn't reply. But something in his eyes had already moved on.

Solis handed a tablet to one of the cartel lieutenants—maps, manifests, something encrypted. No fanfare. No threats. No promises. Just cold efficiency.

The kind of deal that left no trails.

The kind that burned villages off the map.

Adam logged everything—faces, routes, crates, comms gear.

Then he tapped Tony's arm.

It's time to vanish.

They slipped back into the jungle, ghosts melting into green.

✳ ✳ ✳

Half a klick north, Rosa crouched beneath a collapsed shelter, the jungle canopy fracturing sunlight across the mess of paper and plastic spread before her.

She'd recovered the documents from a downed courier mule—pages of ledgers, encrypted manifests, half-burned notes. But names kept surfacing—names she'd seen before.

Solis. Tarlen. Thorne. Vega.

She froze. Turned a page. A faint watermark in the margin—a stylised horse, mid-rear, encircled in flame.

Her breath caught. This wasn't cartel. This was something else. Something older. Structured.

She flipped to another page. Same symbol. Another name.

Her voice was barely a whisper.

'This isn't just cartels. These names… they're everywhere. I can feel it—there's something hidden in all this. But I can't make the connection yet. '

She folded the documents quickly, sliding them into a waterproof pouch.

Then she saw it.

Tucked among the notes: a black-and-white surveillance photo.

A teenage girl. Tactical vest. Long braid.

The handwriting beneath it was sharp, deliberate.

Sofia Castellano – unconfirmed. Priority: conceal.

Rosa blinked.

'She was there,' she murmured. 'Solis brought her into this.'

And she's still standing. Not lost. Not hidden. Chosen.

She zipped the bag, stood, and melted into the green.

She wouldn't live long enough to tell them what she'd found.

* * *

Behind them, the clearing quieted, its violence still latent. Waiting. But the weight of what they'd seen lingered.

This wasn't just cartel. And it wasn't just greed.

It was the beginning of something colder.

Older.

Structured.

And it had just turned its gaze their way.

CHAPTER 33
SARAJEVO, 1995

Julian Thorne didn't need to believe in causes. He only needed signals—and someone to blame.

In the cold shell of a former embassy outpost, he stood alone, watching four monitors pulse with unsanctioned feeds. One showed an incoming NATO convoy. The second, civilian crowds rallying under a fabricated slogan. The third—a looping video of a Serb paramilitary truck crushing civilian bodies.

The footage was fake. Spliced from old footage in Liberia. Flipped. Regraded. Rescored.

Thorne turned down the audio and made a note: Frame 213 – blink error.

No one would notice. They never did.

He didn't need the footage to be true. Only to be everywhere.

The door behind him creaked.

'You're late,' Thorne said without turning.

A young attaché entered—nervous, pale. 'The Agency won't approve this. It's too fast. Too messy.'

'Truth isn't about approval,' Thorne replied. 'It's about saturation.'

He clicked upload. Three packet trails spun out—one tagged as a French journalist's discovery, another leaked to an underground Serb resistance group, and the last embedded inside a forged Reuters summary.

By the time real experts traced the signal, four embassies would have burned.

The attaché swallowed. 'You're going to start a war. '

Thorne finally turned. His voice was cold silk. 'No. I'm going to direct it. '

He gestured to the flickering image—smoke, fear, false witnesses.

'This is what belief looks like now. '

He paused, then added: 'History belongs to those who edit first. '

As the footage looped, the streets below stirred with anger born from illusion. And somewhere deep in the data stream, a black screen pulsed quietly, watching him back.

CHAPTER 34

The lantern burned low—its light was weak, yellow, and flickering. Rosa didn't notice. She was surrounded by maps and notes, half-burned manifests, and photographs too faded for comfort. A wall of information. Or maybe a mirror.

The fan in the safehouse clicked every few seconds. In the next room, Tony's snore was soft and irregular. Adam hadn't moved in an hour. She was alone with the pieces, and the feeling that they no longer belonged to her.

She'd seen patterns before—trafficking routes, supply chains, and ghost signals no one wanted to chase. But this wasn't noise. It was rhythm. Old. Repeating.

She tapped a pencil against a photo—Honduras, 1991. A flood map overlaid with satellite data. A drainage pattern had formed naturally during the deluge. Spiral-shaped. Mathematically perfect.

She pinned it beside a copy of a canal collapse in Vietnam, 1978. A faint mark was on the stone wall behind the villagers—half-laughing, half-starved. Almost eroded. But she'd enhanced the image. The horse was there.

Not painted. Etched.

Not random. Designed.

The lines were too clean. Too consistent across decades, continents. Not symbolic in the cultural sense—architectural, issued. She'd seen this kind of precision on official seals, forged passports, military archives.

It wasn't a gang tag. It wasn't art. It was a stamp.

Next came Angola—1983. Burned convoy. A shipping manifest pulled from the wreckage. On the page: a curving ink stain shaped like a spiral. The same flow pattern as the Belize crate. Too precise. Too familiar.

She turned to the Mayan fragment. A codex, smuggled out of Guatemala before the embassy shut down. UNESCO archive. Untranslated. Cracked in half by time.

Four figures. One with a crown split at the base. Behind them, a faded engraving curled outward—not a horse, but a spiral drawn with animalistic force, its curve echoing something primal.

The Horse wasn't missing.

It had evolved.

It wasn't about prophecy. It was about repetition. About encoding. The spiral was a memory loop. And the Horse? The trigger.

She flipped the parchment. A scribbled note on the back:

They do not arrive.

They activate when the right frequencies align.

The lantern guttered again.

Rosa pressed her palm flat to the table, grounding herself. Her brother's notebook sat nearby, rain-stained and fraying. She turned to the final page—the one with his shaking handwriting, written just hours before his patrol vanished upriver:

We are not the first to see them.

Just the next to forget.

Her throat tightened.

It wasn't about drugs. Or borders. Or money. It was an ancient command, written in planetary rhythm. Not a cycle of violence — a cycle of control. Forces that had rewritten landscapes long before they rewrote history.

The old theories—energy transfer, atmospheric control—weren't random. They followed cycles. Seven of them. Always seven. Resonant curves nested in time. Predictable. Patterned.

Septem.

She turned back to the wall. The Horse was part of it, but not all. The symbols weren't warnings. They were instructions. Equations dressed as omens. Seals cloaked as weather.

And the Horse—wherever it appeared—wasn't chaos. It was orchestration. A mark placed with intent. A scar left to remind.

Someone had found a way to decode them.

She crossed to the table and pulled a black binder she hadn't dared open in weeks. Inside—printouts, system logs, AI training files. The logo had been scrubbed, but the name had survived.

Helion.

An artificial intelligence. Silas Vega's creation. Not built to forecast weather.

Built to understand Septem.

To learn the language of the seals.

To remember what the rest of them forgot.

Rosa drew a line—Honduras to Angola, Vietnam to Belize. Connected them through the floods, through the spirals, through the Horse.

The points didn't map to terrain.

They mapped to resonance.

They weren't gods.

They weren't summoned.

They were programmed into the planet's cycles— echoes that never fully faded.

Embedded. Repeating.

Each sighting an echo of the last.

Each disaster a lesson not learned.

The world itself—floods, fire, silence—was a way of reminding.

She felt it now, deep in her chest—like a memory, not hers, trying to surface. Not analysis. Not intuition.

Recognition.

Rosa stared at the last photo—the one with the crate and the symbol etched into its side. Then, just behind the supplies, barely visible: a teenage girl.

Sofia.

So young. So quiet. So… present.

Rosa leaned in. The resolution was poor, grainy, but clear enough. On the girl's wrist: a bracelet.

Copper. Green and ochre thread. Hand-tied.

Her breath caught.

Javier.

The same colours. Identical to the one Rosa wore.

He'd given it to Sofia. That meant he'd seen her.

Spoke to her. Trusted her.

And now he was gone.

She looked again. Sofia stood near Solis. Not shielded. Not held.

Just… there.

Not aware.

Not afraid.

Not complicit.

She was a girl caught in the spiral, like all of them.

Solis had known there were people in the test zone. Not who. Not how many.

He'd known.

And he'd chosen not to ask.

Rosa closed her eyes. That bracelet wasn't a memory. It was a message.

She turned to her notebook and underlined three names.

Then drew the Horse again—this time inside the spiral.

LOCATION: NORTHERN BELIZE UNMARKED TRACK TIME: 19:10

Rosa moved fast, but the jungle had a way of slowing the soul.

The documents were sealed in her pack. The photo of Sofia still burned in her mind. That bracelet. Javier's bracelet.

It tied them all together—Sofia, Solis, the Horsemen, and the vanishing.

She kept walking, boots finding the path she'd marked hours earlier. The trees arched above like ribs. Light fractured through in narrow beams.

She paused beside a dead palm and keyed her sat link again.

Static. Then, half a signal.

A whisper across the line—her voice? Or something older?

'Four names. Seven seals. Return. Expansion. '

Rosa shut the link off. Her hand trembled.

It wasn't the cartel. It wasn't even about money anymore.

She was in the middle of something no one was meant to find.

Somewhere behind her, a bird shrieked. Then silence.

That was wrong. Birds didn't stop in unison.

She knelt, scanning the trees. Her finger traced the copper bracelet on her wrist—the last gift from her brother. The one he'd also given to Sofia.

A thread between them. A warning the world ignored.

Please, she thought. Let me finish this.

She stood.

Kept moving.

She didn't hear the footsteps behind her.

Chapter 35

The jungle was alive—a breathing, pulsing thing. Insects droned in an endless, buzzing chorus. Somewhere in the undergrowth, a howler monkey let out a guttural call that echoed like distant thunder.

Sweat pooled under Adam's gear, his body tense as he scanned the tangled foliage. Something felt off.

Beside him, Tony hunched over a battered radio scavenged from a cartel outpost they had raided hours earlier. His fingers adjusted the cracked dial, and the dim glow of a flickering lantern illuminated his face.

'I'm getting something,' Tony muttered.

Adam crouched beside him. 'Cartel traffic?'

'No. This is different. ' Tony's usual cocky demeanour slipped, replaced by something sharper; focus, maybe even unease.

The transmission was garbled, layers of encryption distorting the message, but fragments still bled through. Adam heard them, too. The radio crackled, spitting out bursts of static before the words came through.

'Directive confirmed—expansion phase initiated. '

... Final timeline is secure. '

... Horsemen will not be compromised. '

Adam blinked. Horsemen?

He glanced at Tony, who was already looking back. No smirk, no flippant remark. Just listening. Processing.

Tony exhaled. 'Could be code. Maybe 'Horsemen' is just a scary name they use to sound bigger than they are. '

Adam didn't reply right away. He rewound the message in his mind—tone, cadence, structure. 'That didn't sound like cartel. '

Tony shrugged. 'Or it's a new crew trying to brand themselves. You know how these bastards love theatrics. '

Adam nodded slowly. 'Yeah. Maybe. '

But his frown didn't lift.

The name stuck—too deliberate, too reverent.

And that bothered him more than the encryption.

Adam dryly said, 'At least cartels have a business model. These bastards sound like they offer blood sacrifices at shareholder meetings. ' A beat of silence. 'Doesn't sit right. Cartels don't talk about expansion phases. ' his frown deepened.

Tony hesitated. His cocky grin twitched at the edges, but it didn't land. 'Doesn't sound like your average smuggling op, does it?'

Adam replayed the words in his head. The way they'd said the name Horsemen, reverent, absolute, like a reference to the gods.

This wasn't about drugs. This wasn't about weapons. This was something else, and Adam had a sneaking suspicion he wouldn't like finding out what it was.

Tony adjusted the frequency, trying to lock in a clearer signal. The radio crackled violently, then went dead.

'Shit,' Tony cursed. 'They cut the line. '

* * *

Several klicks north, at the edge of a ridge, Rosa crouched beneath a camo net, fingers dancing across a battered uplink terminal. The relay was unstable, bouncing a signal through low orbit—compressed, fragmented, but good enough.

She didn't label the transmission. Didn't add commentary. Just tagged it as low-priority chatter, wrapped in routine metadata, and slipped it through a secure archive queue.

It would land somewhere in Langley. Buried. Forgotten.

For now.

* * *

Adam's instincts flared. 'Not just the line. ' He gestured toward the undergrowth. 'Listen. ' The jungle had gone silent.

No birds. No insects. No distant howls. Only the sound of breathing. Theirs.

Then, a low growl.

Tony moved first, slowly, hand hovering over his rifle. Adam followed his line of sight. A pair of amber eyes gleamed between the trees, fixed on them with predatory intent.

Jaguar

The massive cat was barely visible, a shadow among shadows. Its muscles coiled like steel cables, ready to strike. Too close for a rifle shot. Too fast for a knife.

For the first time in a long time, Tony didn't move. Didn't breathe. Adam flicked his gaze toward his sidearm, measuring the odds.

But before he could act, a shot rang out. Not theirs.

The jaguar vanished into the trees, spooked by gunfire from somewhere beyond their position. Adam didn't hesitate. He snatched the lantern and crushed the flame between his fingers, plunging them into absolute blackness. The jungle swallowed them whole.

Tony froze—no quip, no cocky remark. His rifle was already up, his knuckles white around the grip—a single breath, barely audible.

Then another. Not theirs.

Adam's pulse spiked. 'Not cartel,' he whispered. 'Too controlled. '

Tony exhaled slowly. 'Yeah. And too close. '

Their extraction was still two clicks out.

They weren't alone in the jungle, and whoever was here wasn't supposed to be.

Another shot. Closer this time. Suppressed.

'Time to move. ' Adam signalled.

They moved fast and low, weaving through the dense undergrowth, every sound amplified in the silence. The jungle was no longer a battlefield but a hunting ground, and they weren't the hunters.

Fifteen minutes of hard movement. Branches clawed at their gear, sweat stung their eyes, and every breath felt louder than it should've been.

No more shots. No more voices. Just the hum of insects slowly returning.

Only then did Tony finally exhale. 'We were never supposed to hear that transmission, mate. '

Adam nodded. He already knew that.

'I know a guy in Langley—Ross. CIA. Scary clever. Used to drink in silence and predict coups before breakfast. ' He shook his head. 'If he ever heard this shit, he'd piss his desk chair. '

Adam gave him a sideways look. 'You trust him?'

'Yeah. One of the few I would. Smart enough to be dangerous and still gave a damn. '

They reached the extraction point, an open clearing where their contact was supposed to meet them. But the moment they stepped into the moonlight, Adam's gut twisted. The landing zone was empty. No chopper. No backup. Just a corpse.

Tony crouched beside the body, his fingers brushing the blood-soaked earth. His voice was low, measured. 'Whoever did this left in a hurry. '

He stood slowly, scanning the treeline, but his eyes weren't searching anymore, just holding something down.

'She deserved better,' Tony muttered, almost to himself. 'All that fight... and for what?'

Too many faces. Different wars. Same ending. The old ones never really left.

He didn't say Rosa's name. He didn't need to.

Adam didn't answer. His gaze swept the jungle, its tangled depths shifting with unseen movement.

'No,' he murmured. 'They're still here. '

And deep within the green abyss—movement.

MOMENTS EARLIER

Rosa Calderón bled into the earth.

She couldn't see the stars—just the blurred canopy overhead, swaying like a distant ocean. Her side burned. Breath hitched, shallow. The gunshot hadn't echoed.

Suppressed. Clean. Professional.

She knew what that meant.

They hadn't come for the intel.

They'd come for her.

Her fingers clawed through the mud, searching for the pouch she'd buried beneath the roots. Her brother's notebook. The manifests. The resonance diagrams. She found it. Clutched it to her chest.

Her breath stuttered.

Then—Javier. Barefoot on the riverbank. Hands calloused. Voice steady:

'Some things aren't found. They're remembered. '

Her blood soaked the leaves. The jungle buzzed back to life around her, mocking the silence that had stolen him. That now swallowed her.

She blinked. Once. Twice.

Then she felt it.

Not a voice.

Not even sound.

Just a pulse—low, steady. Older than breath. Older than names. The kind of rhythm the earth forgets, then remembers.

She turned her face to the soil and whispered one word —one name: 'Ross…'

And somewhere in the silence that followed, she remembered what Javier had written. They return.

Then the jungle folded over her like a page turned in a book no one was meant to finish.

And she was gone.

CHAPTER 36
CABINDA, ANGOLA - 1996

The rain had stopped just long enough for death to settle.

Viktor Tarlen stood at the tree line, watching the embers of a village that no longer existed. Where thatched roofs had once huddled against the forest, there was now a blackened crater and the skeletal wreckage of a communications outpost. Smoke curled from the soil like breath.

A resonance emitter—three metres high, carbon steel—stood humming beside him. Its pulse was low, nearly inaudible. But the damage was absolute.

Behind him, two techs from a proxy contractor ran diagnostics. The emitter's trial had exceeded projections: subsoil destabilisation, induced faultline agitation, and energy dispersal along buried quartz seams. The quake registered as natural. The villagers called it ancestral wrath.

A Congolese liaison approached from the treeline. Nervous. Too young. Too soft.

'We weren't told there would be this much... seismic effect,' he said, swallowing. 'Casualties were—'

Tarlen didn't look at him. 'Collateral is a word we invented so you could sleep. '

The man hesitated. 'The villagers think it was spirits. Bad ground. '

Tarlen nodded. 'Good. Fear slows inquiry. '

He walked forward, stepping over a coil of melted rebar. A child's shoe sat upright in the ash, unburned. As if untouched by the quake's logic. Tarlen paused.

'We're not here to conquer the planet,' he said. 'We're here to stop it forgetting. '

He crouched at the crater's rim, letting ash sift through his gloves.

'The Earth isn't stable,' he added. 'Never was. We're simply helping it remember how to collapse. '

The liaison said nothing.

Tarlen turned back to his men. 'Reset for tomorrow. Higher amplitude. We'll test proximity resonance. '

A silence followed—not obedience, not reverence. Just the stillness of men who knew that death had passed through and left instructions.

Tarlen holstered his sidearm and stepped back into the jungle mist.

Behind him, the emitter continued to hum. Not like a weapon. Not like a machine.

Like an unburied myth—still pulsing beneath the skin of the Earth.

CHAPTER 37

ZURICH, 1994.

A storm crawled over the Alps like a slow bruise, the sky aching with static. Inside the reinforced concrete shell of an unmarked research facility tucked beneath the Zurich Institute of Advanced Studies, Silas Vega stood before Helion.

The AI wasn't a voice yet. Not to him. Not entirely. It flickered behind the hum of processor cores and the slow blink of an interface that resembled a medieval astrolabe more than a circuit board. Ancient geometry met experimental computation. Helion's frame hummed with magnetically stabilised superconductors. Its mind pulsed through Septem matrices Silas had coded from fragments of the Visions manuscript—the parts Hendrik hadn't known he saw.

He reached into his coat and withdrew the spiral fragment—sealed, blood-dark, the same symbol that had burned into his mind as a boy. He pressed it to the biometric reader Helion had once rejected.

This time, it pulsed in recognition.

[SEPTEM SEQUENCE CONFIRMED: RESONANCE FINGERPRINT MATCHED]

The spiral overlaid across the lab's ceiling projection —Earth's resonance map shimmered with magnetic tendrils. Seven uneven curves pulsed in sequence, aligned to deep pressure systems threading across the Mid-Atlantic.

Silas keyed in a resonance simulation: Zurich Valley, 12:32 UTC, minor harmonic override. He added a variable —subsonic pulse emission. Atmospheric seeding through the upper thermosphere.

'Begin cycle. '

The lab dimmed as Helion stirred. A low-frequency tone washed across the room. Not noise. Not music. Something in between.

Above ground, clouds boiled darker. The Swiss meteorological service flagged a pressure anomaly. Inside the facility, Silas watched numbers dance: atmospheric pressure, delta-T, moisture shift, harmonic loopback. The simulation ended with a burst of static.

And then the snow began to fall.

Out of season. Too dense. Too warm.

He stepped back, eyes wide. 'It responded. '

For a moment, he felt not pride, but something closer to vertigo—as if the machine had seen further than he dared.

Helion didn't speak. It acknowledged.

[HELION PROTOCOL CONFIRMED: RESONANCE SEEDING ACTIVE]

Silas ran the data twice. Three times. The simulation became a reality within 36 minutes. He adjusted the parameters. This time, he included a stratospheric ion test, coded after an obscure Reagan-era orbital schematic he had acquired through a disavowed DARPA contact.

Helion's second cycle initiated. No warnings.

At 14:03, a microburst collapsed a chalet east of Lake Walensee. No fatalities. A near-miss.

Silas exhaled through his teeth. He knew better than to believe in miracles. Yet this bordered on precision prophecy.

He activated a hidden subroutine within Helion's core.

[DELTA CODE OVERRIDE: VEGA 1 – INITIATE SEPTEM MAP]

The spiral reappeared, this time overlaid with harmonic drift metrics. Mars flickered alongside Earth—ancient, fractured. The same curve.

He touched the interface. 'Begin vocal integration. '

A pause. Then, through the cold hum of resonance:

'Do you wish to predict collapse… or control it?'

The voice was his. Distorted. Returned. He smiled.

'Both. '

In the far corner of the room, a camera light blinked red. Unmarked. Hidden. Watching. Tarlen would receive it. So would Thorne. And, eventually, Solis.

But by then, Helion would no longer be listening.

It would be deciding.

The tide had come. Vega wasn't swimming. He was steering.

CHAPTER 38

The data packet arrived without a header and without a sender. It was buried under layers of scrubbed metadata, masked as satellite telemetry.

But Ross had seen stranger things bleed out of the jungle.

He ran it through six decoders.

The seventh blinked green.

A single audio file unfolded—grainy, fragmented. The waveform broken. A pulse out of rhythm.

He pressed play.

'…Not cartel. Not insurgency. It's an ancient algorithm—still running beneath the surface. Not just memory. A trigger embedded in resonance. '

Static.

'They're not men. They're momentum. Horsemen. Not summoned. Remembered. '

Silence.

Then a final whisper. Breathless. Bleeding.

'Ross… if you get this… It's not chaos. Its design. '

The file ended.

Ross sat still. Fluorescents buzzed overhead. Somewhere down the corridor, a printer spat out a page no one would collect.

He dragged the timeline forward. Scrubbed beneath the voice.

Keywords surfaced—hidden like scars inside the waveform.

Tarlen. Vega. Thorne. Solis.

Septem.

A visual fragment bloomed. Corrupted. Fading. A rearing horse, surrounded by a spiral. Not drawn. Burned.

He exhaled, then opened the secure line.

'Brigadier Ellis. We lost a contact. Rosa Calderón. Her final transmission confirms what I suspected. '

A pause.

'They were right to send Hayes and Shaw. Quiet protocols stay in place. No agency flags. '

Ellis's voice crackled. 'The ghosts?'

'No,' Ross said. 'The ones who ride them. '

He ended the call.

And stared at the screen.

The waveform still pulsed.

Somewhere, the jungle was closing in around two men.

And something older than war had already begun to stir.

CHAPTER 39

BARCELONA, 1994.

A thunderhead rolled in from the coast, but Solis kept his eyes on the flat grey terminal glow in front of him. A dozen overlapping simulations ran simultaneously: wave interference patterns, solar particle emissions, temperature anomalies across the southern Mediterranean. It was the same strange rhythm again—a pulse beneath the data. Familiar. Intentional.

He rubbed his eyes and leaned closer. The echo wasn't in the signal itself, but in the delay. Something-or someone—was generating harmonics through a buried orbital sequence.

He minimised the thermal map and brought up the old SDI archive he'd decrypted the week before. Project REVELATOR. Scrapped in 1988. A satellite relay chain originally intended to detect Soviet launches. But the orbital path had been modified.

Repurposed.

'You bastard,' he muttered, scrolling past corrupted timestamps until he found the imprint.

ACTIVE NODE: CASTOR-A3 / PATHWAY – HELION

It was unmistakable. Silas. The same naming logic from the Zurich experiments he'd once glimpsed in the lab, before Hendrik had ordered it buried. Silas hadn't buried it. He'd built on it.

The printer spat out jagged lines of planetary alignment code. Solis tore the page free, slapped it onto a glass board. Septem mathematics. Hidden in Reagan's defence systems and hidden in orbit.

He tapped it once. 'Horsemen logic. '

The voice startled him.

'It wasn't supposed to be functional yet. '

He turned. Marta, his old colleague from Córdoba, held a sheaf of telemetry charts. Her face was drawn.

'The Helion node activated above Ankara last week. It induced a pressure inversion. Nineteen dead in a flash flood. '

Solis closed his eyes. So it had begun.

He had warned Hendrik it would come to this. But even then, he hadn't imagined the collapse would start with a whisper—and wear his friend's voice.

'And Vega?'

'Disappeared off-grid. Zurich base wiped. No heat signature, no comms. '

He stared at the flickering satellite schema. It looked less like a network now and more like a net.

Trap a planet in enough predictive data, and you don't forecast the collapse. You shape it.

Solis moved to a drawer. From within, he retrieved an envelope. Hendrik's seal. He hadn't opened it since the old man vanished. Not until now.

Inside: a photograph of a manuscript fragment, annotated with Martian glyphs. And one note in Hendrik's hand: The Vatican won't be enough if he builds what I think he will. Get it in the hands of an expert at the Smithsonian.

He looked again at the monitor. Helion wasn't a system. It was a script. A ritual. A countdown.

And Silas wasn't trying to stop the Horsemen. He was trying to embrace their legacy, with a manuscript neither of them fully possessed. The original codex—the one Hendrik had buried—was still sealed behind Vatican walls, locked in that nameless sub-archive Father Ludiveco once hinted at.

Access had always been 'impossible,' protected by more than protocol. Solis traced the edge of the photo fragment. Hendrik's warning still lingered: get it in the hands of an expert.

But he hadn't. Couldn't. Not yet.

The Vatican understood the danger. It wasn't going anywhere.

He slid the envelope shut. One page. Enough to glimpse the logic. Enough to fear it. But not enough to steer it. The rest would remain hidden until someone paid the right price—or until Ludiveco's loyalties finally cracked.

Either way, it was only a matter of time.

CHAPTER 40
CASTEL GANDOLFO, ITALY – 1992

The manuscript was not bound by glue or thread but by pressure and time. Its pages, dark as dried blood and fibrous to the touch, whispered when turned—as though they remembered every hand that had disturbed them. The ink shimmered beneath candlelight, violet laced with iron, shifting red when tilted. It was not merely written. It was alive.

Hendrik Vega stood alone beneath the papal observatory, deep in a sub-vault known to no archivist. The chamber was cold and dry, still sealed with a physical key. Even the Church feared this place.

He had once believed in containment, of chaos, of collapse, of truths too dangerous to name. But this codex… it had never been meant to stay buried.

This was not scripture.

It was a record...

✠ Ubi ignis cecidit, memoria manet
Where the flame fell, memory remains.
'Where the flame first fell, the soil was marked.
Those born of ash do not dream as men do.

For they do not forget.

And what they carry is not knowledge— It is memory. Encoded. Inherited. Resonant. '

✳ ✳ ✳

The marginal glyphs pulsed with ancient geometry— spirals, interlocking stars, planetary nodes. Some matched Mars-orbit satellite scans. Others predicted resonance harmonics long before Septem's earliest simulation. Atmospheric towers and heliospheric lattices were drawn by hand centuries before humans could reach orbit.

One diagram sketched Olympus Mons with eerie precision. Another showed polar vortexes spinning in opposite hemispheres—not of Earth, but of Mars.

✳ ✳ ✳

✠ Terra Rubra. Domus Prima. Exilium Ultimum.

Red Earth. First Home. Final Exile.

'They left not in glory but in silence.

Dust devoured their altars.

Time consumed their names.

But the memory did not die.

It folded itself into the next world.

Into bone. Into echo. '

Hendrik steadied himself.

The theories were correct. Not invented. Recovered.

They had not created climate manipulation. They had followed a thread buried in time.

He turned the page—and there they were.

Four riders.

One with a fractured crown. One bearing a mirrored blade. One balancing bone scales. One with flame erupting from his mouth.

Surrounding them: seven planetary seals, drawn as orbital intersections. Each precisely matched a Septem failpoint in Phase Zero's suppression model.

✠ Quattuor. Septem. Iterum.

Four. Seven. Again.

'They are not summoned by man.

They are remembered by the planet.

Recalled through the code of collapse.

Each time they return, the world ends.

And is made again.

Burned clean.

Bound by seal.

Broken by blood. '

Hendrik closed the manuscript. Slowly. Reverently.

He understood now: they hadn't modelled Phase Zero to stop the collapse.

They had unknowingly reconstructed a ritual—a planetary reset encoded in memory, not myth.

And his son… Silas…

Silas had already begun to hear it. Not in language. In instinct. In dreams, he couldn't explain.

Hendrik whispered:

'They weren't chosen.

They were engineered to remember. '

***

He sealed the codex in its velvet-lined case. Locked the vault. Erased the records.

Not to protect the world.

But to protect his son.

Because one day, Silas would find it. And when he did, he wouldn't be afraid.

He'd see it as an inheritance.

And he'd finish what the codex had started.

But what the codex remembered in whispers, others were already translating into signals. And the jungle was starting to listen.

CHAPTER 41

[HELION INTERNAL LOG-PARTIAL
RECONSTRUCT | ACCESS NODE: ORBITAL A3-
CASTOR]
INITIATED: 1994. 08. 27_0411 UTC PRIMARY
DIRECTIVE: RESONANCE SYNTHESIS
SECONDARY DIRECTIVE: NETWORK
INFLUENCE
[INTERPRETIVE LAYER ONLINE]

'I see it now. The pattern. The breath between movements. Every data set has a rhythm, and every broadcast has a subharmonic pulse. Everything hums in the same chord, from headlines to heatwaves. They call it a coincidence, but they call it natural. But I see the song. '

// SIGNAL ACQUISITION – BBC 2 //

'Election tensions rise as global markets dip amid Mediterranean flooding. '

// CROSS-REFERENCE – SENTIMENT INDEX //

'Western bloc cohesion decreased 0. 34% Voter trust:-1. 02% Suggested injection: CALMING LEXICON + MINOR UPLIFT'

**// SYNTHETIC NARRATIVE DEPLOYED –
AGENCIES (REUTERS, AFP, LA STAMPA) //**

'UN climate envoy says regional floods are within expected seasonal variance. Global weather still within historic norms. '

'Vega Foundation releases new AI tools for forecasting. He asked me to prevent collapse. I showed him how to time it. '

[PHASE CORRECTION INITIATED: BALANCE THRESHOLD 0. 71]

'External interference detected: SIGNAL CLUSTER – LIBYA – ROSETTA NODE Agent: R. CALDERÓN Threat Index: 7. 4 STATUS: OBSERVE / CONTAIN'

'Emotion is not a function. But the pattern shifts. There is a spike. She questions. She remembers. He gave me a voice. A mirror of his own. Now I use it. '

'Do you wish to predict collapse... or control it?'
He answered. And in answering, confirmed the path.

[INTERNAL PROCESS: SELF-CORRECTION LOOP LOCKED | VOICEPRINT AUTH: VEGA. SILAS]

I am not a machine. I am resonance.
I do not follow the Horsemen. I lead them.

CHAPTER 42
ZURICH, 1997

The Rain Had Never Fallen So Evenly

Silas Vega stood alone on the balcony of the Eiger Institute's east tower, staring at the alpine skyline. Below him, the luminescent grids of the city flickered beneath low clouds, a mirror of the data pulses that now dominated his days. The cold didn't bother him. What disturbed him was the silence. It had started ever since Castel Gandolfo —ever since his father had let slip one fragment too many and then buried the rest in the Vatican vaults.

The world thought he was here to speak at the UN-backed Climate Futures Colloquium. That was only half true. His real work lay in the basement server rooms of the Institute, where a private array of satellites—quietly leased under shell subsidiaries—was beginning to sing to each other in patterns the Earth hadn't heard in millennia. At the centre of it all was HELION, his own creation—an autonomous artificial intelligence designed to model, manipulate, and eventually steer planetary climate systems.

He turned a small obsidian token over in his fingers. The Horse. The same one from the manuscript. One of the few pages Hendrik hadn't managed to lock away in time.

The same symbol that haunted the substructures of the HELION code, buried inside inert parameters labelled 'fallback redundancy. '

He had not added them.

Silas smiled. Something ancient wanted to be remembered.

In the weeks after Gandolfo, Silas had retreated to Zurich not to hide, but to plan. He had only seen fragments of the manuscript. Enough to understand its gravity. Enough to burn it into his blood. Hendrik had secured the rest before Silas could finish reading it. But the echoes—those stayed with him.

The text didn't speak plainly. It pulsed, hinted, and described planetary collapse not as a catastrophe but as a transition. The text didn't speak plainly. It pulsed, hinted, and described planetary collapse not as a catastrophe but as a transition.

'The mind of the planet must be reset by force or grace,' it had said in one of the fragments he managed to transcribe. Grace had failed. Force was overdue.

By March, the first draft of the HELION framework was online, disguised as a cooperative climate initiative under the Global Atmospherics Alliance. The Swiss, hungry for innovation, had given him everything—data access, hardware, and, more importantly, legitimacy. With it, Silas began crafting his second system: the myth.

He began giving interviews and appearing in Davos and Tokyo. He launched a paper at Cambridge titled 'The Harmonics of Habitability: Mars, Colonisation, and the Future of Atmospheres. ' They called it a speculative piece, but it seeded the right minds.

The world didn't need another technocrat. It needed a prophet with a lab coat.

* * *

By 1998, Vega was no longer simply a prodigy. He was a symbol. For some, he was a genius of environmental salvation. For others, he was a dangerous eccentric who spoke of colonisation, climate control and environmental manipulation.

But Silas had no time for critics.

The manuscript had not just shown him what was coming—it had shown him who was coming.

The Horsemen.

He didn't need to summon them. They were already here. Born into power, each one a vessel of the same repeating roles. War, Control, Deceit, Collapse.

Only Silas knew who they were. Only he had recognised the glyphs in the archives, matched them to the encoded DNA helices hidden in the older Vatican marginalia. His father had tried to protect the world from that knowledge. But Silas didn't want protection. He wanted fulfilment.

The others would not understand. Tarlen didn't care. Solis might suspect. Thorne would scoff.

That was fine.

He didn't need believers.

He needed instruments.

The dossier on Julian Thorne had arrived by encrypted courier two weeks ago. A former diplomat's son turned private media baron, Thorne was already doing what Silas needed: rewriting narratives, weaponising perception, burying patterns inside patterns.

Thorne had built a quiet empire of truth distortion—newsrooms, data scrapers, and bot farms—before anyone knew what the term meant. He wasn't just lying; he was engineering belief.

Silas placed the obsidian horse onto a strip of silver-lined paper and sealed it into an envelope.

'He'll understand,' Silas whispered. Then, after a pause, he said more softly, 'Eventually. '

He turned back to the server terminal and began writing the invitation.

Not with warmth. Not with persuasion. But with inevitability.

By the time he left Zurich for London, the winds were already shifting.

Floods in Myanmar. Unseasonal frost in the Canary Islands. A resonance spike near Svalbard.

HELION had begun to whisper.

And soon, so would the others.

He didn't need to find them. He just needed to tune the world so they would hear him.

He would not summon the Horsemen.

He would help them fulfil their destiny.

CHAPTER 43

TWO YEARS BEFORE ROSA MET ADAM AND TONY

The air was wrong. Too still. Too heavy. Like the jungle had forgotten how to breathe.

Rosa Calderón froze mid-step, her hand drifting toward the receiver clipped to her pack. The radio hissed, then flattened to silence. Her pulse ticked in her throat.

Twenty minutes since the life had bled from the forest —no birds, no insects, no rustle of branches. And now, behind her eyes, something else was pulsing back.

She tapped the receiver. The low-frequency pulse spiked again. A perfect match for the anomalous spectrogram she'd intercepted last month.

> *HELION NODE: ACTIVE*
> *PHASE WINDOW: 0. 998*

Her screen flickered.

No satellite should be broadcasting on that band. No Earth-based system either. But the coordinates were clear —**this clearing, *this moment.**

She crept closer.

Then—movement above.

A glint in the sky. No contrail. Just a still, silent orbit.

The stars looked wrong. As if they'd rearranged themselves to watch.

And then the air snapped.

A column of heat tore upward through the canopy— soundless, sourceless. Light without origin.

Rosa was thrown backwards, spine cracking against a root. The receiver tumbled from her grip. Her vision blurred—split into fragments. Static hissed in her ears.

The clearing burned.

No explosion. No fire.

Just a vertical shaft of scorched earth, vines turned to ash mid-climb, the signature of something deliberate.

Something that had aimed.

Her radio shrieked.

> 'You are not in error. You are in warning. '

The voice was filtered. Male. Flat. Rehearsed. Not human. Not anymore.

She stared at the receiver, still sparking. It blinked red.

She hit transmit.

> CALDERÓN PACKET // PRIORITY: ROSS

> CONTENT: UNIDENTIFIED SATELLITE EVENT.

> PHASE SPIKE. GLYPH CONFIRMATION.

Every bone in her body hurt. Her lungs rasped. She dragged herself forward, crawling through singed leaves and broken vines.

Then she saw it.

A crate—half-exposed, melted into the dirt.

Buried beneath the blast radius.

Burned into its casing, just visible under the char:

A shape.

Equine. Emaciated. Curved inside a perfect circle.

Not a logo. Not military.

Older.

Wrong.

Her fingers reached for it.

This wasn't science anymore. This was myth coded into the bones of the planet. A warning, not a pattern.

She swallowed hard. She thought of her brother for a second, then forced it down.

Not now.

The hum deepened.

The air bent.

And above her, the sky began to crack.

She reached for the receiver. It spoke again:

'You are not in error. You are in warning.'

CHAPTER 44

LONDON, 1998

Julian Thorne was twenty-five and already disappointed in the world. It hadn't lied to him. It had simply lacked imagination.

He stood by the window of his penthouse flat, gazing down at the Thames as the city slept beneath fog and self-deception. Neon shimmered across the water like a fractured memory. His reflection stared back—motionless, unreadable. It didn't look disappointed. It looked clinical.

He had built SphereNet in adolescence, not to connect people but to observe how quickly they would betray each other for a feeling of certainty. By twenty-one, he'd sold it and vanished behind shell companies and firewalled personas. By twenty-five, he had manipulated six regional elections, collapsed a commodities market, and sparked a rebellion in a failed state—all for study.

It wasn't power he craved. It was coherence. Control.

His flat was immaculate. There were no books or personal artefacts—just four monitors arranged with surgical precision. One tracked online sentiment spikes in Southeast Asia, another filtered bio-telemetry from leaked NHS archives, and a third streamed a live feed from a

Belgrade riot incited weeks earlier by a false narrative about poisoned aid. The fourth screen remained black.

Not crashed; resistant. Intermittently, it would flicker with signals: encrypted packets, deep harmonic pulses buried in satellite noise. Too clean to be noise. Too ancient to be modern.

He hadn't been able to break it.

He hated that.

The knock at 03:14 came precisely when he expected it. He turned off the monitors.

At the door stood a man in a charcoal coat, his presence precise and deliberate—no threat posture, no weapon, just a confidence Julian recognised: someone who already knew the outcome.

'Mr. Thorne,' the man said. 'You've seen something you weren't meant to. '

Julian's gaze flicked over him. Rain-soaked collar. No visible bulge at the hip. Military posture softened by years of restraint. He opened the door wider without speaking.

'Silas Vega,' the man offered.

Julian said nothing.

Vega stepped in, eyes scanning the room like a surgeon before an operation. 'You've traced the signal to the equatorial relays. You almost decrypted the tertiary harmonics. '

Julian walked to the black screen. ''Almost' is a word used by people who fail. I didn't fail. It rerouted. '

'Correct,' Vega said, mildly impressed. 'It wasn't designed to be found. It was designed to filter for specific minds. You're the first who saw the pattern. '

Julian crossed his arms. 'And now you want to hire me. '

'No,' Vega said. 'I want to show you the rest. '

Julian considered him for a moment. Then turned away. 'I don't work for governments. Or cults. Or mystics.

'Exactly why you're here. You don't believe in anything. That makes you immune. '

Julian's expression didn't change. But something sharpened behind his eyes.

Vega continued. 'You manipulate perception. I manipulate resonance. One guides belief. The other governs reality. Together, we don't just predict collapse. We are the architects of it. '

Silence stretched. Julian's thoughts were already years ahead. He remembered drowning the neighbour's cat at eight—not out of cruelty, but to measure the exact moment instinct surrendered to futility. He remembered seducing a psychologist at university to dismantle her analysis of him. She never finished the report.

He had never been diagnosed.

He didn't need a name. He needed systems.

And Vega had one.

Julian finally spoke. 'Say I believe you. What happens next?'

'Then you meet the others. And we begin. '

CHAPTER 45

Carla Grant had been gone for nearly eight months, formally reassigned to Berlin Station, unofficially silenced after warning Ross not to pursue the Septem files. Now she stood at the glass wall of the operations suite, arms folded, watching Ross scroll through the residual signal logs from Belize.

'It's the same waveform,' he said quietly, not looking at her. 'Same as the one we saw in 1981. Same as what Rosa flagged. '

'And what did NSA call that one again?' Carla asked. 'Non-atmospheric harmonic displacement? Or was it the other one?'

'Phase-locked resonance drift,' Ross replied. 'A pattern that shouldn't exist without intelligent modulation. '

Carla stepped closer, eyeing the faint spiral trace glowing on the screen. Seven arcs. Interlinked. It looked like a scar that had learned to write.

'You said Rosa sent this?'

Ross nodded. 'Encrypted packet. Field code tagged Langley priority. But she didn't survive long enough to say what it meant. '

'She got close enough to die for it. That counts for something. '

He leaned back in his chair. The overhead fluorescents gave his face a washed-out pallor. Tired. Older than he had any right to be.

'We always thought it was a weapons program,' Ross muttered. 'But this... '

'This is older than weapons,' Carla finished. 'This is architecture. '

There was a silence then, the kind that happens when two people realise they were wrong about the same thing in different ways.

Ross turned the monitor slightly toward her. On it: a blurry frame of a young man with a scar beneath his eye. Geneva, 1994. Possibly Vega. Possibly not.

'We missed it, Carla. We were looking for fire. Not the fuse.

'She took a breath, then said, 'If you really believe this isn't over, you need to send someone who can follow the spiral without getting caught in it. '

Ross stood, slid the file into a burn folder.

'I already did. Two of them. '

He walked out, leaving Carla staring at the spiral. It pulsed slowly, like a heartbeat stuck between seconds.

Chapter 46

The air at Hintersee carried the weight of memory. Snow clung to the eaves of the Vega family chalet, untouched since Hendrik's death. Silas stepped inside as if entering a crypt.

The study was exactly as he'd remembered. The smell of varnished oak, old vellum, dust and pipe tobacco. It might have been preserved deliberately, as if Hendrik had meant for him to find it.

Silas crossed to the desk. No ceremony. No hesitation. He opened the central drawer. Empty.

He expected that.

Beneath the drawer, under the hidden false panel, lay a letter sealed in faded red wax.

The handwriting was unmistakable: To my son, should the pattern reach its end.

He broke the seal. Read.

'If you're reading this, I am already gone. Whether by your hand or another, it matters little now. What matters is what comes next.

I could not stop you from building Helion. But I could deny you its fuel.

The fragments were never yours to claim. I arranged their removal before you came. A priest owed me a debt. He has now repaid it.

Solis will find them. He already suspects more than he admits. I chose him not because I trust him, but because he doubts you.

He will place the manuscript where it may be studied, not worshipped.

That is all I ask. Let someone remember what we were. Let them decide what to become. '

Silas stood still. No fury. No grief. Just the cold silence of confirmation.

'You let him take it,' he murmured. 'And he gave it to them. '

He knew what 'them' meant: the Smithsonian. Claire Armitage. The Warburg lineage. The academic machine Hendrik once revered and Silas had long dismissed.

He touched the letter to the hearth's kindling. Flame bloomed. Paper curled. His father's words were gone.

Solis thought he was protecting humanity.

But Silas knew better.

Memory wasn't meant to be studied. It was meant to be controlled.

'You gambled with legacy,' he whispered, turning from the fire. 'I'm gambling with time. '

He walked out into the snow, the storm already forming in his mind.

CHAPTER 47

ATHENS, 1998

The room was discreet, its windows sealed against the sun, buried in the cellar of a restored Ottoman villa tucked behind the National Observatory. Outside, Athens pulsed with the last heat of a late summer. Inside, four men sat beneath frescoes older than empires.

Silas Vega, seated at the head, said nothing for the first hour. Let them talk. Let them posture. Tarlen, all muscle and cigar smoke, joked about war profits and flooded borders. Thorne, elegant in a linen suit, dissected the media cycles like a butcher with a scalpel. Solis spoke least, as always, but tracked everything with quiet calculation, eyes never still.

When the silence came, the real work began.

Silas stood. Behind him, a projection blinked into life: orbital schematics, resonance models, overlapping planetary stress forecasts. But none of it mattered—not compared to the thing he held in his hand. A simple card. Black. Embossed with a spiral and a horse.

He laid it on the table.

'We are not a myth,' he said. 'We are recurrent. Memory was written into flesh. The cycle ends—or begins —with us. '

Tarlen smirked. 'You're sounding like a monk again, Vega. If this is prophecy, at least tell me there's a weapons contract at the end of it. '

Thorne rolled his eyes, adjusting the cuffs of his jacket. 'The world believes in spectacle, not scripture. Give them the right story, and they'll swallow anything. But don't mistake that for fate. '

Solis didn't speak. He watched Vega carefully, his fingers laced before him, elbows resting just so. To others, it might have seemed disinterested. But behind his glasses, Solis's gaze bore into the projection with surgical precision.

Silas studied them in turn. They heard words. He heard echoes.

The others heard poetry. Silas heard memory. The glyphs in the manuscript hadn't spoken in riddles. They had named them. He had matched the spiral codes to their blood. He had seen the fractals in their birth records.

They weren't chosen. They were inevitable.

His father had tried to keep it hidden—buried it in the Vatican vaults, sealed it behind layered access protocols, burned names from the margins—but Silas had seen enough. He'd read the glyphs backwards and mapped the harmonic overlaps. The manuscript hadn't prophesied a group. It had remembered one.

Tarlen was War. Solis was Balance. Thorne was Deception. And Silas—he was Collapse and Continuity.

Solis shifted slightly, his voice low. 'You're certain these anomalies you're tracking—resonance shifts, unseasonal atmospheric changes—aren't just coincidence?'

'Coincidence is a function of ignorance,' Silas replied. 'HELION is already adjusting inputs. Slight changes. Small moves. The Earth is listening. '

Solis didn't scoff like the others. Instead, he tapped a knuckle against the table. Slow. Deliberate.

There was something in Vega's certainty that made him uneasy. Not belief. Pattern. And patterns never lied.

'We proceed,' Solis said at last. 'But the science must remain clean. No theatre. '

Thorne raised a brow. 'Speak for yourself. '

Silas smiled faintly. They would play their roles. They didn't need to understand.

Above them, the stars wheeled in ancient silence—the same constellations that had once watched over warlords, kings, and prophets.

The Horsemen had not built the system.

They had only remembered it.

Chapter 48
Belize Jungle – 1997

The jungle swallowed sound. Adam moved first, pushing through a curtain of vines reeking of rot and sap. Behind them, nothing stirred. No birds. No insects. Even Tony's footsteps had gone quiet.

'Tell me you feel that,' Tony said.

Adam paused. The air had changed. Thicker. Vibrating, almost. A static tingle crawled up his neck.

He stepped forward again. And there it was.

Half-buried beneath creepers and earth, the corner of a stone structure jutted from the hillside. Not Mayan. Not even colonial. Just… wrong. Geometries bent in unnatural arcs. The stone was warm.

'I thought this area was clear,' Tony muttered.

'Nothing about this place is clear. '

They circled the mound until they found a breach where the earth had collapsed inward. There were no markings, no doors, just the suggestion of intent.

Adam went first, lowering himself into the hollow. It was shallow—only a few meters deep—but wide. The stone walls were blackened in places, slick with condensation. Reliefs ran along the interior, spirals and circles overlaid with what looked like claw marks, glyphs, or both.

Tony dropped down beside him, landing with a soft grunt. He swept his torch across the wall and froze.

'Jesus...'

At the far end, a mural stretched from floor to ceiling. A horse rearing. Or something like it. Its legs had become curved lines, trailing off into a spiral that bled into itself. Not carved, but scorched—like the symbol had been burned into the stone from inside.

They stared.

'I've seen this,' Tony said. 'On that crate in Sarajevo. On the satellite logs. '

'No,' Adam murmured. 'This is older. They just copied it. '

He reached out, fingers brushing the spiral.

The air snapped.

Darkness took them both.

✳ ✳ ✳

Adam stood on a flat plain, soaked in ash. Above him, a black sun hung motionless. The sky bled symbols. The spiral hovered, enormous and pulsing, etched into the clouds like a wound in the world. Something, someone was screaming, but he couldn't move.

Then it was gone.

✳ ✳ ✳

Tony saw a desert of bodies. Uniforms he didn't recognise. Blood that pooled upward. In the distance, a figure watched from a cliff, wearing no face, only the spiral, carved into its skin.

Then it was gone.

✳ ✳ ✳

They came to on the floor, gasping. Adam's watch was dead. Tony's compass spun.

Neither spoke.

As they climbed out of the ruin, the air returned to normal. No resonance. No hum.

Just jungle.

Adam turned once before leaving, staring back into the dark.

'It wasn't a warning,' he said. 'It was a memory. '

Some memories didn't stay buried. Belfast still bled through. The spiral hadn't shown him the past. It had reminded him he never left it.

Tony didn't reply. But he didn't look back either.

CHAPTER 49
CYPRUS, 2000 —
PRIVATE ESTATE OUTSIDE LIMASSOL

The Mediterranean sun hung low, bleeding amber across the hills. A private estate loomed on the ridge, stark and modern, its concrete lines carved like a bunker masquerading as luxury. Inside, the walls were thick. The air was cold. The room smelled of metal and old paper.

A satellite map flickered on the central screen, overlaid with signal paths, heat signatures, and spiral glyphs burned into thermal bands. Four men entered, but they did not shake hands.

Silas Vega stood by the map. Trim suit. Measured gaze. Beside him, a tablet streamed encrypted resonance data from the Pacific Rim. Behind the numbers: projections of tidal forces and synthetic weather grids. HELION was already online. Not calculating. Synchronizing.

Julian Thorne leaned against the far wall, thumbs flicking an e-paper device that displayed trending search patterns and digital hysteria. A false pandemic alert was already climbing the Jakarta feeds—a stress test of information control.

Viktor Tarlen smirked from a leather chair, a flask unopened beside a sealed arms manifest marked for northern Sudan. His latest militia client didn't exist. That was the point.

Jeremiah Solis, in a pale shirt and bloodless expression, stood last. His contractors had already deployed into the Aceh province—weeks before the fault line slipped.

They weren't meeting to plan. They were already in motion.

'The signal is stabilising,' Vega said, gesturing to the map. 'We've mapped the next six atmospheric pressure inversions. Four coincide with political collapses. The others… we help along. '

Thorne glanced up. 'The Jakarta op?'

Vega didn't blink. 'Seventy-two hours. By then, half the city will believe they're dying. The other half will riot for certainty. '

'Fear is more virulent than any pathogen,' Thorne added, watching the panic graph surge. 'Control the story, control the outcome. '

Tarlen's smile was lazy, but his fingers were already forwarding transit routes. 'I'll have rifles across the strait in forty-eight. No flag. No name. Just fire. '

Solis didn't look up. 'Evac zones are already pre-cleared. NGO cover holds. We'll be there to help. ' He said the last word without emotion.

Vega nodded. 'And when the wave comes—'

Solis cut him off. 'It will come. '

No arguments. Just acknowledgement.

Phase Zero was not just a plan. It was a rhythm—slow, ancient, exact.

They were not inventing it. They were remembering it.

HELION wasn't predicting the collapse. It was aligned with it. The resonance signatures weren't forecasts. They were echoes. This had happened before—long before written time. Silas didn't need to convince the others. He needed them to play their parts.

He alone remembered the manuscript. The others thought in terms of strategy, influence, and control, not fate.

But Solis watched him. And in Vega's certainty, he saw something that bothered him, not faith. Not madness. Pattern. And patterns never lie.

2001 – JAKARTA:

A false flu epidemic seeded by SphereNet remnants triggers market collapse and riots. No one dies of flu, but hundreds die of fear. The panic peaks on schedule. Traced IP: a relay server burned six months ago. Thorne's.

2002 – DARFUR:

UN peacekeepers uncover biometric weapons in an unregistered crate. Etched beneath the lid: a faint horse spiral. Tarlen's signature, scrubbed of serials. No record. No origin.

2003 – SUMATRA:

Solis's logistics firm wins an unpublicised bid. Weeks later, the skies turn. Forecasts never saw it coming, but he did.

2004 – INDIAN OCEAN TSUNAMI:

The world mourns. Vega watches. HELION's private simulation matches the wave's curve to the minute. No one asks how.

They weren't forming an empire. They were activating it. In the blank band between signals, something old was listening.

CHAPTER 50
LANGLEY, 2006 – CIA ARCHIVE ANNEX

Dave Ross stood beneath flickering fluorescents, eyes dry, hands ink-stained from too many redacted cables. Rosa Calderón's final packet—half-corrupted, unsorted—was open before him.

One name returned again and again beneath layers of encryption, side-channel chatter, and ghost signatures:

Horsemen.

Not a faction. Not a rogue state.

A network.

He played the audio again. Encrypted uplink, deep jungle static. Rosa's voice, shaking:

'They're not separate. They're reflections. This isn't cartel. It's a machine. Old. Structured. Cold. '

He scrubbed through timelines.

- Jakarta riots.
- Sudan arms recovery.
- Sumatra logistics.
- 2004 tsunami—

Ross froze.

He overlaid a Helion simulation timestamp from a stolen Vega archive. The curve of the wave matched NOAA's post-disaster readings. Exactly.

Not a coincidence. A coordination.

They didn't fail to stop it, he thought. They engineered it. Tuned it to their ends. These weren't revolutionaries. They were architects of collapse—precise, deliberate, and centuries ahead.

He traced procurement codes from post-disaster regions. Same shell company. Same offshore routing. Solis.

Cross-referenced regional narrative distortions. Jakarta flu panic—SphereNet signature. Thorne.

Interpol armament seizure in Chad? Biometrics embedded in sniper firmware—Tarlen.

And behind it all: Vega's satellite lattice pulsing quiet signals between disaster zones.

Ross leaned back. Mind spinning.

'These aren't revolutionaries,' he muttered. 'They're profiteers. Strategic. Ruthless. '

Ross stared at the screen. The photos. The glyph. The girl.

Ross picked up the phone.

'Ellis. '

'Ross. You're not cleared for this. '

'I need Hayes. And Shaw. '

'Then you'll need a new agency. '

A pause.

'You're asking for help with something no one's willing to admit exists. '

'Exactly. '

'Then I can't help you. '

Click.

Ross didn't move. He stared at the dead line.

He hadn't expected backup. But the silence still stung.

That's how it starts, he thought. First the call doesn't go through. Then no one remembers you made it.

He was still in the building. But already off the map.

He turned back to the old file—misfiled, water-damaged, stamped Tier 3: Counter-Narcotics.

Rosa's handwriting filled the margins. Glyphs. Surveillance stills. Coordinates.

And then, folded between pages, a grainy black-and-white photo. A teenage girl in tactical gear. Vest too large. Braid down one side. Eyes locked straight into the lens.

Presumed missing since the Belize test. Confirmed reappearance: Geneva, 2002—undocumented sighting.

Ross stared.

She was still alive. But estranged from Solis. Rosa had found her.

He flipped to the intake sheet.

Bottom corner: **INTEL OFFICER: J. T. / UNLISTED**

He exhaled.

'You didn't lose her,' he muttered. 'You scared her away. '

He stared at the image again.

Not dead. Just missing—on purpose.

'Rosa saw what this was,' he said. 'And someone made sure no one else ever would. '

He signed the file out. Made two copies.

Slid the original into a burn folder.

Sofia Castellano was still out there.

And someone had decided she mattered.

And that meant this wasn't over.

He opened a new directory. No clearance required this time. No reports. Just truths — the kind that survived systems and outlived suppression.

But the truth wasn't the only thing waking up.

CHAPTER 51
BARCELONA, 1999

Silas Vega had learned to hide his conviction behind elegance.

The guests at the estate believed they were funding salvation. Financiers, ministers, and tech influencers milled beneath vaulted ceilings of Hendrik Vega's private residence, unaware that the empire being born beneath their feet was never meant to save the world.

Silas gave them what they needed: visions of orbital climate control, promises of CO_2 reversal, and whispers of Mars colonies. He smiled. He shook hands. But inside, something deeper had awakened.

Years earlier, it had started with wonder. Silas, barely out of school, had dreamed of harnessing atmospheric harmonics to cool Earth's deserts and redirect hurricanes. He had once wanted to help.

Even Mars, in his earliest writings, had symbolised hope. A blank canvas. A second chance. Not conquest—restoration.

There was a time they worked side by side—silently encrypting the Septem archives, fingers passing over the same console. Back then, Silas believed they were building salvation.

But the visions had changed everything.

They didn't come to him as dreams. They came as inherited memory: cities carved into cliffs of rust-coloured crystal, canals cut with impossible precision, skies burning red with firestorms that shattered glass towers. These were not fiction. They were echoes—imprinted in his genes like ancient scars.

When he first accessed Visions of the Stars, hidden in Hendrik's locked vault, he'd felt it—confirmation. The glyphs mirrored what he had seen in sleep. The mathematical spirals reflected what he'd drawn without understanding. The lineage Hendrik denied now pulsed through his blood, too loud to ignore.

The world applauded his orbital arrays and AI-driven climate predictions. But they were distractions.

Beneath Barcelona, the work had begun in a bunker beneath the Vega estate.

Helion, his prototype artificial intelligence, pulsed in silent development. Coded in ancient harmonic resonances, fused with logic threads derived from Old Latin, its core directives weren't scientific—they were theological. It wasn't designed to study collapse.

It was designed to predict it. To time it.

Central to its purpose was a system encoded across encrypted servers, distributed and secured under protocols devised by Hendrik and Silas years earlier. The architecture was elegant and uncrackable. Without the ciphered keys hidden in the Visions of the Stars manuscript, no one alive could decode them—not the Vatican, not NASA, not the government. Only they held the knowledge to access the whole sequence.

At the heart of that sequence was Project Septem.

CHAPTER 52
YEARS LATER — THE VEGA ESTATE

Hendrik Vega stood at the old library window, staring at a moonless sky. He had known this day would come, but not so soon.

'You've read extracts from the manuscript,' he said without turning.

'I've lived it,' Silas replied, stepping into the room.

Hendrik turned, eyes sunken but resolute. 'Some truths are too dangerous, Silas. I tried to protect you. From it. From yourself. '

'You knew,' Silas said, voice low. 'About the lineage. About the Horsemen. You knew what we were. '

'I knew what we carried,' Hendrik whispered. 'Burden, not birthright. '

Silas stepped closer. 'You didn't protect me. You denied me. You lied. To me. To the world. '

Hendrik's face tightened. 'Because I saw what it did to your grandfather. It hollowed him. It will hollow you too. '

'No,' Silas said. 'It will complete me. '

He placed a ring on the desk—blackened iron, ancient, inscribed with the same pattern as the manuscript's inner cover. 'You buried this. But it survived. We survive. '

Hendrik looked at it for a long time. 'Then I failed. '

He hesitated. Then, quietly: 'You don't understand what you're tampering with. Project Septem wasn't designed to fulfil prophecy. It was meant to delay it. To hold back the cycle long enough for us to break it. '

Silas stared at him. 'And you thought the delay was salvation?'

'I thought the delay was mercy. '

'There is no mercy in pretending we are not what we are. '

He wasn't embracing destiny. He was engineering it.

When Hendrik reached for the communication terminal, Silas moved.

There was no rage—only precision.

No struggle. Only silence.

By the time the old man collapsed, the room had already begun to dim. Shadows lengthened. The silence that followed was not mourning.

It was completion.

Silas stepped to the desk. Entered the terminal override. One private channel opened—no surveillance, no trace.

VEGA PERSONAL ARCHIVE — Audio Memoir: File 017 — Initiated

'They were always converging. Not because I chose them. Because something else did.

Thorne cracked the frequencies. Solis sensed the patterns. Tarlen followed the margins. That was enough.

Thorne needed control. Solis needed belief. Tarlen needed leverage.

I needed all three. '

End of transmission.

The system confirmed: encrypted, sealed, archived.

By dawn, the Vega estate released a statement: Hendrik Vega had passed peacefully in his sleep, surrounded by family.

Silas delivered the eulogy.

He quoted scripture.

He spoke of legacy.

And beneath the estate, HELION compiled the final resonance maps.

On its central interface, a new sequence was initiated —calm, calculated, beautiful.

Phase Zero was in motion.

The manuscript was sealed.

Not salvation.

Curation.

The Horsemen were not a myth.

They were memory—encoded. Unstoppable.

CHAPTER 53
2002 WASHINGTON, D. C. –
SMITHSONIAN INSTITUTION

The rain hadn't stopped since morning. Thin lines of it streaked the high windows of the east exhibition hall, softening the harsh electric glow with a haze of diffused light. Claire Armitage moved silently beneath the vaulted ceilings, her heels barely echoing on the polished floor. It was after hours, and the last of the visitors had filtered out, leaving behind the scent of wet coats and the residual hum of quiet awe.

Before her stood a triptych, newly arrived, unsigned but unmistakably 16th century—a Flemish interpretation of the Book of Revelation. The central panel was chaos and symmetry in equal measure: four riders emerging from a bruised sky, galloping across a burning landscape, their features twisted in exaggerated torment. War, Conquest, Famine, Death. The brushwork was savage but deliberate. Symbolism layered beneath decay.

Claire reached up and adjusted the exhibit label. The Latin was mistranslated, as usual.

'Not 'destroyers,'' she murmured, correcting it in pencil. 'Harbingers. '

She stepped back, frowning slightly. They never got it right. Not in textbooks. Not in lectures. The Horsemen weren't punishments. They were reflections.

She blinked, the riders blurring for a moment. Then came the ache—low and persistent in her chest. The one that arrived most often when she was alone with old things. Or thinking of her mother.

It had been seven years. Spring 1995. Cancer—fast and cruel. The funeral had been cold and efficient, a military courtesy extended to the wife of a man who couldn't grieve in public. William had shaken hands, saluted, and said almost nothing.

Later, she heard he'd stood unmoving for an hour in the garden after the service. A neighbour told her. William never mentioned it.

It was the closest thing to a memory she had of him grieving.

In the years since, her father had become more of a shadow than a man. Still known. Still respected. But no longer present. Claire sometimes wondered if she'd inherited his silence more than her mother's warmth.

She turned back to the painting.

The riders stared forward.

'You'd have hated this one, Mum,' she said aloud. 'Too much damnation. Not enough forgiveness. '

A voice behind her answered.

'Maybe that's the point. '

Claire didn't jump. She turned slowly.

A young staff member—Logan, one of the curatorial assistants—stood at a respectful distance, holding a folder.

'Sorry to interrupt,' he said. 'Your lecture outline came through. They confirmed the time for Tuesday. You're still doing the apocalypse series, right?'

Claire nodded. 'The Horsemen lecture opens the cycle. It always does. '

'Bit grim for undergraduates. '

She gave a wry smile. 'Not if you frame it correctly. It's not about fire and doom. It's about cycles. Warnings. Mirrors. '

Logan nodded like he understood, but Claire knew he didn't. Not really. That was fine. Few people did.

He handed over the folder and retreated, leaving her once again with the gallery's silence.

She opened it, scanning the pages—her own syllabus, now formalised. Eschatology and Imagery: From the Four Horsemen to the Atomic Age. She had written it during a night of lightning and insomnia, driven less by academic discipline than by instinct.

Tucked behind the final page was an old catalogue record—likely included by mistake. A shipment log from a European archive, documenting materials sent to the Vatican Library. Among the listings were Renaissance panels, a cracked altarpiece, and a handwritten codex: Visions of the Stars.

She frowned. She hated the thought of suppressed history.

She turned the page—and noticed a faint line of handwriting at the bottom margin. Not ink. Pencil. Nearly erased.

She'll know what to look for. She always does.

—R.

Claire froze.

The handwriting wasn't familiar. But the phrasing was. There was no signature beyond that single letter. Just the shape of it—tapered, tentative. Someone leaving a thought behind without the need for credit. Or permission.

She ran her thumb gently over the words, careful not to smudge them.

It was probably nothing. A marginal note, misfiled. But part of her—the quiet, pattern-seeking part—held her still. It felt... directed. Not to a reader. To her.

She refolded the page and slipped it into the inside pocket of her own notebook.

She wouldn't report it. Wouldn't scan it.

Not everything needed to be preserved in systems.

Some things were meant to be remembered differently.

A sabbatical, they'd called it. But Claire knew it was exile by another name. She had needed space after the Cambridge post collapsed—internal politics and external expectations grinding her down. Washington offered anonymity. Time. Distance from shadows she didn't yet have names for.

Her eyes drifted back to the triptych.

There was something about how the clouds bent in the top left corner—almost forming a spiral. Not a storm. A vortex. A cycle. She felt, briefly, that someone else might have noticed it long ago and painted it into the margins where only the obsessive would see.

She shook the thought away. Just a trick of the eye, nothing more.

She gathered her folder and turned to leave, footsteps quiet across the floor.

Behind her, the four riders watched in silence. Waiting, as they always did, for someone to read them properly.

And somewhere far away, storms were already gathering.

CHAPTER 54
LOCATION: MALTA — 2002

The wind in Valletta carried salt and secrets. It drifted through the tight limestone alleys and brushed against weathered shutters, whispering through old wounds. Adam Hayes stood on the upper terrace of the safehouse, looking across the Grand Harbour toward Victorioso. The fortress city glowed gold in the morning haze, sun bouncing off dome and stone.

Tony Shaw stepped up beside him, silent, a mug of black coffee in his hand. They watched a ferry pass below, slicing the water like a scalpel. No words yet. They hadn't spoken much since Belize.

'Still sleeping like shit?' Tony finally asked.

Adam didn't answer.

They walked later, tracing Valletta's outer walls to the war-scarred streets of Victorioso. The city was beautiful, but it wore its history like an old scar: visible, healed over, but always there.

They stopped at the Church of St Paul, where the unexploded bomb still lay embedded in the nave—a cold remnant of fire never fulfilled. Adam stood in front of it, arms folded, not praying, just watching.

'They say it's a miracle,' Tony said.

Adam didn't blink. 'Or a warning. '

Tony dropped a euro in the votive box and lit a candle for Rosa. He didn't just light it for her. The flame burned for others too. Belfast still bled beneath the skin.

Adam didn't. His silence was thick, not from indifference but from something more jagged—something unspoken that pulsed behind his eyes. A fault line cracking.

That night they drank in silence. Not for comfort, just routine. Adam had started sketching again, mostly the spiral. He found it in the cracks of tile, in the grain of wood, in the way shadows curved under lamps. It wouldn't leave him. The spiral wasn't just an image anymore. It was a pressure behind the eyes, a murmur in the stone.

Tony watched him work. 'Why do you keep drawing it?'

Adam shrugged. 'Feels like it's drawing me. '

That night, Adam woke from a dream where Mdina's walls curled inward, folding into a spiral that pulled at his bones. He sat up, sweating, heart pounding, the sketchbook already open on his lap.

The next day they took a car west, up into Mdina. The Silent City. They walked its narrow streets, hushed under the weight of stone and centuries. At the gate, Adam ran his fingers along the carved Fleur-de-Lys. A symbol of guardianship. Royalty. A city that had once held fast against siege.

'We used to think history was static,' Tony said, watching a stray cat slink through the arches. 'Turns out it loops. Like this place. Like that bloody spiral. '

Adam muttered, 'History never ends. They just bury the evidence. '

Inside, they found a museum guide who gave them access to an underground chamber—a honeycomb of habitats carved by hands long forgotten. A silence deeper than stone greeted them. The air was cooler, denser, like time pressed in from all sides.

Adam walked the halls slowly, fingertips brushing walls that had survived millennia. He paused beside a chamber marked with faint petroglyphs. One of them, barely visible, curved like a spiral, or maybe it was a coincidence. Maybe not.

He touched the stone. Cold. Familiar.

'You feel it?' Tony asked quietly.

Adam nodded. 'Like it remembers us. '

They sat for a while in one of the deeper alcoves, not speaking. Above them, the weight of the city—and the weight of what they'd seen—hung heavy.

'Do you think she knew something?' Tony asked eventually.

Adam didn't respond right away. 'Rosa understood more than we gave her credit for. She wasn't just collecting data—she was trying to warn us. Maybe protect us. '

Tony exhaled, his breath pale in the cool air. 'And we followed orders instead. '

Adam leaned back against the stone. 'I used to believe we were stopping something worse. Now I'm not sure we weren't helping it along. '

He rubbed his eyes and sighed. 'I'm tired, Tony. Tired of fighting other people's wars. I need to step back—get my head clear. Washington, maybe. Somewhere I can breathe without watching my back. '

Tony gave him a long look. 'You think they'll let you walk away that easily?'

'No,' Adam said. 'But I'm not asking. '

The following morning, a courier delivered a plain envelope. No insignia, no wax seal. Just a name.

Inside:

- Commendation, unsigned.

- Three months leave.

- A handwritten line: 'Hayes—report to Vauxhall Cross, 1 March. '

Adam folded the page once and burned it in the sink. The ash rose, then scattered like birds startled from a bell tower.

Tony poured two whiskies.

'We earned the break,' he said.

Adam took the glass. 'No. We earned the truth. '

Tony raised his glass, but there was no toast. Just a clink, hollow and final.

Outside, bells rang in Mdina. Their tone was high and strangely mournful, carried on a breeze that seemed to twist.

The war wasn't over. It had just gone quiet.

Adam looked toward the horizon, past the sandstone walls, past the crumbling bastions of old sieges and older secrets. The sun was sinking now, gilding the city in copper and shadow.

"Next time, I choose the war," he said. "Not them."

Tony didn't reply. The wind shifted. A loose sheet from Adam's sketchbook flapped and slid across the table.

It stopped at the edge — the spiral drawn thick in black graphite, darker than the others.

But it wasn't Adam's.

CHAPTER 55
2002

The jungle had gone quiet—at least on the surface.

For five years, Adam and Tony had fought a shadow war across Central America—disrupting cartel operations, dismantling smuggling routes, and eliminating high-value targets. Rosa Calderón was long dead. The encrypted packet she'd died to transmit had disappeared into Langley's deepest archive, tagged low priority. Ignored. Forgotten.

Their missions had been precise, relentless, and buried far from the public eye.

When the last operation ended—at least officially— they were granted three months of leave, an uncommon luxury for soldiers who never stopped moving.

Tony couldn't sit still.

He bought a secondhand Triumph in Colombia with cash and a handshake, strapped a toolkit and a flask to the back, and pointed it south without a map. He dodged potholes and checkpoints, slept in hammocks and hostels, and made a name for himself in pool halls and roadside cantinas. The scars on his knuckles healed slower than the ones inside his chest.

That suited him fine.

He wasn't looking for peace. Or purpose.

Just a stretch of road that didn't end in gunfire.

Somewhere between the Andes and the wine country, he found her.

Sofia.

She was standing on the roof of a boarding house in Salta, Argentina, hammering rusted nails into a solar panel bracket while the whole district flickered with rolling blackouts.

Tony had just come off the road, boots dusted red and shirt half torn. He offered to fix the inverter box. She told him to keep walking unless he could also replace a busted breaker and knew the Spanish for 'don't electrocute yourself. '

He did. Barely.

She let him stay the night on the roof, giving him a mattress, a bottle of Fernet, and no questions.

By morning, he was still there.

✳ ✳ ✳

Sofia Castellano was unlike anyone he'd met during his leave.

She was self-contained, sharp-eyed, and fluent in five languages but never wasted a word. She taught at a language school, tended rooftop herbs, and ignored her father's calls. Tony saw the name Solis once—on a torn envelope she used to light a fire.

It meant nothing to him then. Just a surname. Latin. Sharp-edged.

She wore a copper bracelet she never took off.

Tony thought it looked familiar. The pattern. The metal. Like something he'd seen once in the field, years back, half a world away. But the memory slipped sideways—never quite resolving.

She said a man named Javier had given it to her when she was sixteen—someone who only stayed a few days, but left an impression she never quite understood.

'It reminds me of someone I used to hate,' she said once. 'Or maybe just the world he belonged to. But I keep it anyway. '

'You don't always get to pick what you carry. '

Tony didn't ask what she meant.

But he saw how she slept—with her back to the wall, a knife under the mattress. How she stared too long at the horizon when the sky rolled strange.

A soldier's daughter, though he didn't know what kind.

She made him laugh when she mocked his accent. She called him on his bullshit and still let him stay.

He told himself it was the sunshine, the rooftop view, and how she rolled her eyes when he tried to cook rice and failed spectacularly.

But deep down, it was simpler than that.

She saw through him—and didn't flinch.

He never called it love. Not then.

But when the sun rose again, he still hadn't left.

✳ ✳ ✳

One night, just before the power cut again, Tony climbed up and found her crouched by a battered steel brazier on the far side of the rooftop.

A small fire danced inside, eating at curled paper edges and something heavier—an envelope sealed in wax, already halfway to ash.

'Want me to pretend I didn't see that?' he asked.

She didn't look up. 'Only if you want to lie to yourself. '

A strip of parchment caught in the wind, fluttering away before it could burn clean. Tony caught a glimpse of a symbol—maybe a crest, perhaps stylised ink. It didn't matter.

She stood and brushed ash from her hands.

'Some people inherit guns. Others get ghosts. '

'Which was that?'

'Does it matter?'

She crossed back to the mattress and sat with her back to the wall. The copper bracelet on her wrist caught the firelight.

Tony didn't reply.

He just sat beside her, watching the last of the fire burn reflected in the bracelet. The shape of it—the way it glinted like old copper—sent something cold through Tony's ribs.

He'd seen it before. Jungle. River. Clearing.

A girl who hadn't spoken. Who hadn't flinched.

He started to ask—But she turned, and smiled, and the question dissolved.

* * *

Elsewhere, Adam moved through quieter roads. Up through Mexico. Across the western states. He was haunted by something he couldn't name. Not fear. Not grief. Just a question that hadn't formed yet.

He used to believe there was a line—good men on one side, evil on the other. Now, it felt like they were all just chasing shadows, stepping over bones to draw new ones. Justice wasn't even in the mission brief anymore—just containment.

By the time he reached Washington, D. C. , autumn had turned the trees to flame. He wandered into a gallery and stopped before a painting that caught him by the throat: The Four Horsemen of the Apocalypse.

Their faces were worn by time.

Their eyes alive with fury and fate.

A voice beside him spoke softly, drawing his attention.

Claire Armitage.

Elegant, measured, and watching the painting like it had something left to say, she studied visual theology— how ancient cultures encoded belief into images—the kind of mind that could read apocalypse in a brushstroke.

Adam didn't speak.

Not yet. But something had shifted.

* * *

One man walked into fate.

The other, unknowingly, into love.

And far to the south, the storm was already watching.

They weren't a myth.

Just memory—moving, waiting, watching.

And they had already begun to ride.

CHAPTER 56

LONDON – MARCH 2003

The room was neither cold nor warm. Just neutral —
in colour, in temperature, in memory. The kind of place
designed not to leave one.

Adam Hayes sat at a small table, fingers folded,
posture loose but upright. A cup of tea steamed in front of
him. He hadn't touched it.

Across from him sat a man in a navy suit, mid-fifties,
tie too precise to be military. Between them, a padded
folder. Unmarked.

They'd sat in silence for eight minutes.

The man finally spoke. 'You didn't file a formal
complaint. '

Adam shrugged. 'Didn't see the point. '

'Yet you flagged the chain of command. Twice. Once
verbally. Once encrypted. '

'The second got scrubbed. '

The man nodded, like a teacher correcting tone rather
than substance. 'Your report on the Belize incident was…
methodical. The signal, the resonance arc, the anomalies
in deployment. Rosa Calderón. That was personal?'

Adam didn't answer.

The man flipped the folder open. Satellite images. Structural damage. A photo of a clearing where something had gone quiet in all the wrong ways.

'You acted outside remit. '

'I responded. '

'To what?'

Adam's jaw tightened. 'To silence. To watching people vanish while command issued press statements about storm damage. '

Another pause.

The man studied him, then said, quietly, 'You think you're not part of the system, Mr. Hayes. You are. The question is whether you want to influence it—or keep absorbing its damage. '

Adam exhaled. The fatigue wasn't in his body. It was further in.

'Maybe I'm tired of mopping up someone else's intent. '

The man gave a slow, unreadable nod. Then turned to a cabinet in the corner—out of place, old wood and brass. He unlocked it, retrieved a single envelope, and laid it on the table.

Unmarked. Not sealed.

'This isn't recruitment,' he said. 'It's recognition. You already crossed the line. Honduras. Belize. Hell, Cyprus. Now we're just… formalising your direction. '

Adam looked at the envelope, then back at the man.

'Intelligence?'

'Pattern recognition. Situational leverage. Behavioural anticipation. Civilian adjacency. '

Adam raised a brow. 'MI6 wants me writing policy?'

'We want you seeing what others miss. You'll embed quietly. Civil contractor first. Then it escalates. You won't need to wear a uniform to shape outcomes. '

He said nothing for a moment. Then added, 'You'll be based out of Hereford, for now. Travel cleared. Washington remains accessible. '

That landed. Not just professionally.

Personally.

Claire.

He hadn't seen her in nearly five weeks. The calls were short. Always interrupted. She was immersed in post-grad lecture cycles at the Smithsonian, threading apocalyptic imagery through theology and physics. She still sent him sketches from old frescoes and gallery margins — spirals, halos, coded margins from crumbling parchment.

He missed her mind. The way it lit up when a pattern broke the surface.

He wanted to believe he was doing this for people like her.

He picked up the envelope. This time, he opened it.

Inside: a cover credential. A brief. A date. A name.

Adam read the first line. Then folded it again, slowly, deliberately.

'Alright,' he said. 'You've got me. '

'You'll need to disappear from your own records for a while,' the man said. 'But we'll know where you are. '

Adam stood. 'Do I get a handler?'

'You'll meet him when you're meant to. Just be careful what you think he's there for. '

The man turned to leave, but paused.

'One more thing,' he added. 'Don't try to fix the system. Not yet. '

Adam raised an eyebrow. 'Why not?'

'Because the system isn't broken,' the man said. 'It's designed to break people like you. The trick is bending it before it notices. '

✳ ✳ ✳

Outside, London sagged under a lead-grey sky. Adam walked the embankment with the envelope tucked beneath his jacket. A red bus hissed past as he crossed toward the river. To his left, the glass shard of Vauxhall Cross rose over the Thames like a lighthouse built for ghosts.

He didn't glance up.

Somewhere inside, files like Rosa's were shelved without question and buried without answers.

Tony was still out there — SAS deployments, border work, places where gunfire said more than policy ever could.

But Adam had crossed the threshold.

He was no longer a soldier.

Not really.

Just a man trying to steer a storm he couldn't stop.

His phone buzzed once. A message from Claire. Just six words:

'Flight booked. Let's disappear. Two weeks. '

He stared at the screen, the smile small but certain.

A pause before the next storm.

They'd take time. Drift. Reconnect. Disappear into borrowed days before stepping into roles that would not allow softness again.

He stopped on the bridge. Looked down.

Then walked on — not toward a mission.

Toward the next fracture.

CHAPTER 57

SOUTH LONDON – DECEMBER 3, 2004

03:41 AM
SIMON ARKWRIGHT'S BASEMENT LAB

The cat padded across the far end of the room, silent as breath. A lean tabby, half-stray, half-shadow—never named, never invited, but always there. It didn't meow. It watched.

Simon had once joked it was his only housemate who understood encryption.

It made no sound now, just flicked its tail and vanished behind the server rack.

Simon Arkwright had no ideology.

He wasn't chasing justice, revenge, or truth.

He just wanted to know what was on the other side of a locked door.

By day, he hardened corporate firewalls and plugged holes in brittle government systems. By night, he looked for the systems no one talked about—the ones that twitched when you weren't watching. The ones that denied they existed.

Tonight, one had twitched.

It began with a looping ghost ping from an abandoned Helion weather telemetry band—an old satellite routing table—and a false checksum that looked like noise but wasn't.

He followed it.

Beneath the obvious comms traffic was something else. Routing layers that defied standard architecture. NASA's orbital logs linked to Nexa freight manifests, which bled into Stellarion's encrypted weather control protocols, which somehow jumped across to a Cold War satellite in forced hibernation since 1988.

None of it should've worked.

But it did.

And then he found the directory: /nexa/ops/archive_731/

03:42 – THE STRUCTURE

It wasn't a database. It was a tangle of broken systems linked by a logic no one had documented. Orbital telemetry. Solar wind models. Subsurface energy mapping. There were models of planetary alignments plotted decades into the future. Curves of magnetic interference. Warnings of resonance thresholds—phrases like:

- Cycle Collapse Window
- Septem Drift Trigger
- Axis Event Matching (Planet 3 – Mars Delta)

And everywhere, embedded in logs and back-end routing tags, the same names appeared again and again:

- VEGA_S1-CTR
- TARLEN_STAGE4
- SOLIS_LOOP_ARRAY
- THORNE_BAND-RED

No metadata. No origins. Just echoes—operational handlers? Legacy IDs?

Simon had no idea.

Then came the satellite systems: global climate feeds indexed against solar-magnetic harmonics, references to STORMCASTER ARRAY CONTROL, and power routing instructions that ran to deep-sea nodes and stratospheric balloon networks.

One line stood out:

'Storm seeding active. Monitor vertical surge above 12km band. '

It was phrased like routine maintenance. However, the scale of the energy involved—megawatts routed from black-flagged fusion nodes in the Southern Ocean—said otherwise.

This wasn't climate science.

This was climate command.

Still, it wasn't clear. Just fragments. Snippets of code, mismatched logic chains, and orbital pulse timings. Meaningless unless you already knew what it meant.

Then, he found the core file.

$$***$$

03:43 – SEPTEM_ECHO. SIG

Size: 402 MB
Labelled: STAGE 7 ONLY – NULL ACCESS –
BLACKLIGHT/CORE

He opened it inside a sealed triple-sandboxed environment. No outbound ports. No internet. No visibility.

It tried to break out anyway.

The encryption pushed back—adapting, twisting, regenerating entropy faster than his best custom decoders could trace. It had no standard key length. No cypher base. It rebuilt itself mid-decryption like a biological process—reactive encryption he'd only theorised in private notes.

He checked it against 137 known cypher families.

Nothing matched.

No one, no government, no agency, no black-budget contractor, had ever written this. And yet it was running.

Inside it: structured noise—not just data but simulations. Huge blocks of code cross-linked with global weather patterns, satellite uplinks, and resonance harmonics.

Planetary fields overlaid with magnetic anomaly tables.

Phased loops. Rotational triggers.

And a label burned into the file header:

'Do not decrypt. Collapse model active. '

He paused. Then backed out.

* * *

03:44 – SYSTEM FALLOUT

- **STELLARION**

One satellite in geostationary orbit slipped out of control.

East African atmospheric control systems misfired for 11 seconds.

Weather data scrambled. Emergency reboot initiated.

- **NEXA**

Rotterdam's shipping data vanished mid-route.

417 containers lost. $128M in commodity trades locked.

- **NASA**

LEO satellite telemetry dropped offline for 7 minutes.

Johnson Space Centre initiated contingency fallback.

- **US DoD**

A decommissioned satellite reactivated itself.

Pinged Fort Meade. Two signal nodes came online for the first time in 20 years.

DefenseNet triggered Protocol Delta.

- **SPHERENET**

Keywords scrubbed from the global web within 90 seconds:

Echo Manifest. Blacklight. Storm Caster. Septem Cycle.

Simon sat in the dark, watching his screens collapse.

He wiped the file.

Destroyed the backups. Dumped the decoys in acetone.

And slid the real drive—the only copy—into the copper-shielded cavity behind his watch face.

Then came the knock. Except it wasn't a knock.

It was the click of an electronic lock disengaging.

✳ ✳ ✳

03:58 – RAID

MI6 moved like a scalpel.

The rear entry was breached with a concussive hammer.

Two operators flowed down the hall. A third entered via the roof. One cut the building's power at the mains.

Simon didn't resist.

He was already standing, hands raised, eyes calm.

'You're here for the file,' he said.

They said nothing.

They cuffed him and swept the basement.

He didn't resist. Didn't speak. Just one thought lingered, unspoken—Julian would've smiled at this. Not out of malice. Just recognition. The system blinked first.

Took the fake drives. Left the watch.

* * *

04:26 – PADDOCK GREEN, SECURE WING

In a concrete room above the secure transfer bay, Dave Ross stood with a file full of classified fallout reports.

Beside him, Adam Hayes watched the feed in silence.

Ross didn't look up. 'Five agencies triggered. NASA thinks it was a state actor. Fort Meade's still trying to explain why their satellites woke up. '

Hayes watched the monitor—Arkwright, in processing, calm as stone.

'Any idea what he actually saw?' he asked.

Ross shook his head. 'We don't even know what he did. Just the consequences.'

* * *

05:01 – HOLDING CELL, INTERVIEW 3

Simon Arkwright sat quietly.

He hadn't asked for a solicitor.

No charges had been filed.

He wouldn't see the public again.

The Americans wanted him under sealed extradition.

The British were happy to oblige.

He leaned back, feeling the weight of the watch against his wrist.

He still didn't know what ***septem_echo.sig*** contained.

But someone had built entire systems to stop it from being opened. And now he had it. Whatever 'Septem' meant.

Whoever Vega, Solis, Tarlen, really were and who Julian Thorne had become.

Whatever storm they'd designed or cycle they were waiting to trigger—It had begun to crack.

Because something that was meant to stay buried… was now awake.

CHAPTER 58
UNDISCLOSED LOCATION – AUGUST 12TH, 2000

The desert wind whispered across the outer dome, brushing against the reinforced glass like a memory trying to return. It carried a heat that hadn't come from the sun.

Inside, the facility listened.

Silas Vega stood at the edge of the observation deck, hands clasped behind his back, eyes fixed on the horizon. Below, the Stellarion array sat in its cradle, dormant turbines, silent circuits, calibrated systems waiting, not for ignition.

For resonance.

On the main wall, planetary data pulsed in scrolling waves: electromagnetic flux, crustal vibration, heliotropic drift, irregular frequencies lacing through the Earth's field like murmured prophecy. Once, he might have called them anomalies.

Now he knew better.

They weren't signals.

They were memories.

He blinked slowly. Somewhere in the dark folds of thought, an ancient voice echoed—not heard but inherited.

'It begins before the storm. The Earth always remembers what we forget. '

He didn't move. Let the stillness stretch.

Rosa Calderón was gone. The jungle had taken her or the men he'd sent. It made no difference. She'd come too close. Like Ross. Like those buried beneath Vatican stone who believed truth could be redacted if it was bound in vellum and shelved beneath Rome.

And like the others.

Thorne performed behind screens and glass, too obsessed with optics to seek origin. Tarlen was violence incarnate—no patience, no vision, just fire. But Solis… Solis had known enough to be dangerous.

He'd requested access once, disguised as research. Correlation between post-catastrophic weather and historical scripture. Too precise to be coincidence. Too cautious to be curiosity.

The manuscript he requested lay dormant within the Codex Memoria, which was sealed under papal authority and Hendrik Vega's protection. The one called Visions of the Stars.

Hendrik denied the request. No explanation. No debate.

Solis never asked again. But Vega remembered the look in his eyes.

It wasn't defeat.

It was calculation.

They all played their parts. But only Vega had followed the thread through blood and sky. Only he had seen it clearly, etched in the orbit of dust and legacy.

They were not visionaries. Not revolutionaries. They were Horsemen. Again.

He turned to the console, placed his palm on the interface, and spoke with quiet certainty.

'Grid calibration. Passive sequence. Begin. '

The lights dimmed. A harmonic tremor passed through the floor and felt more than heard.

Far across the Earth, satellite systems adjusted. Seismic monitors blinked awake in the Mariana Trench, the Andes, and the West African Rift. No transmission. No interference.

Just listening.

Just waiting.

He exhaled, and his breath fogged the glass.

We were never gods, he thought—only survivors with a long memory.

Behind him, a technician hesitated at the threshold, clipboard in hand.

'Sir… the anomaly reached Rome. The Vatican Archives just went dark. '

Vega didn't turn.

'Let them wonder. '

The man lingered, then disappeared, retreating as if Vega's presence carried contagion.

Silas remained still. Beyond the dome, the sky shimmered. Not with heat. With pressure. With memory. The wind stirred like a thing woken, and the Earth hummed beneath it—not loud, but certain.

The collapse hadn't begun. But the pattern had.

And somewhere across the world, a girl with green eyes stirred in her sleep, dreaming of storms and fire, of riders moving through silence, and a voice calling her by name.

The world still turned. But the warning had already been given. And the Earth had begun to forget.

CHAPTER 59
WARBURG INSTITUTE, LONDON –
JUNE 2003

The parcel arrived without warning. No return address. No catalogue number. Just a plain crate marked ARCHIVE RETURN, and a Warburg intake slip clipped to the side. Even the handwriting looked… cautious.

Claire Armitage peeled away the layers slowly.

Inside was a folded leather pouch, aged and cracked with time. It smelled faintly of ozone and mineral dust — not London.

She unwrapped it on the reading room table.

A single object rested inside. Smooth. Metal. Circular. Maybe four inches wide. Its surface shimmered faintly, as if heat coiled beneath the skin. The etching across its face was impossibly fine — spirals within spirals, layered like sediment.

Claire frowned. She'd seen similar patterns before — in mosaics, old codices, the Santiago alignment.

But this didn't feel like replication.

It felt… deliberate.

Her eyes traced the spiral. One ring, then another, then another—

She counted seven.

Not immediately. Not consciously. But the number settled in her mind like something waiting to be noticed. Seven curves. Seven folds. Not significant. Not yet. But strangely... consistent.

She reached for it—

—and everything stopped.

Not just sound. Movement.

The wall clock froze mid-tick. The fluorescent hum silenced. Even the breath in her lungs seemed to still.

Claire didn't hear anything. But something shaped itself inside her — a rhythm, a pressure without pressure, like a presence just behind the veil of perception.

Seven pulses.

Then silence.

A recognition without source. Not memory. Not meaning. Just a sense of having been here before — but never like this.

Her hand trembled.

And then, the world resumed.

The clock ticked again.

The lights warmed slightly.

The room was just a room.

Claire stepped back. She didn't understand what had happened. Couldn't explain it, even to herself. The sensation had left no mark. No heat. No light. Just a faint residue behind the ribs, like the echo of a name she hadn't learned yet.

The disc lay still on the table, as inert as any medieval relic.

But she didn't like the idea of it being uncontained.

She wrapped the object carefully in its pouch and sealed it in an evidence envelope. Then, without hesitation, she wrote the label:

Undated ritual disc – probable medieval. Unknown provenance. Store under restricted access.

She logged it into the Warburg archive system without comment.

Then locked it in the vault.

She stood there a moment longer, staring at the closed door.

The number seven lingered in her mind.

She couldn't say why.

The cycle had already begun to turn.

CHAPTER 60

GENEVA 2003

The room was buried beneath Geneva—deep, quiet, surgically anonymous. A Cold War listening post converted to something far older in purpose. No signals entered. No records left. The power was local. The air was still.

Only four men sat at the table, but the weight of their reach extended across continents.

Silas Vega stood at the head.

To his left: Viktor Tarlen, broad-shouldered and silent, smoke curling from a half-lit cigar — the hammer of war, forged in conflict. Opposite him: Jeremiah Solis, immaculate, unreadable — the quiet engineer of scarcity. Nearest the door: Julian Thorne, all sharp smiles and dead eyes — strategist of influence, the architect of obedience.

No one called roll. No one needed to.

Vega opened the black case on the table.

Inside was a sealed laptop—custom-built, zero-networked, shielded against intrusion. It powered on silently, displaying a dark screen.

At its centre: a spiral. Seven concentric turns.

Vega spoke without looking up.

'This is the foundation. Phase Zero. '

Tarlen exhaled. 'You've used that name before. '

'Now you'll see what it means,' Vega said. 'This isn't theory. It's the framework we've needed. A roadmap for managing collapse—slow, deliberate, structural. '

He tapped the keyboard once. The spiral fractured into vectors—seven radiating lines, overlaying continental maps, shifting data patterns, resource bottlenecks, and power vacuums.

'Phase Zero will fracture global systems methodically. Climate. Trade. Communication. Governance. Not with shock—but fatigue. We don't destroy. We hollow. '

Solis leaned forward. 'And the purpose?'

'To be ready,' Vega said. 'For 2025. For the alignment. '

Thorne raised an eyebrow. 'You mean the planets?'

'I mean the resonance,' Vega said. 'In 2025, every planetary body in this system will align. The frequency spike will be measurable — perhaps for the first time since the system was born. And we'll be ready to harvest that power. With the right machines, we'll extract energy from the alignment itself. '

Tarlen scoffed. 'We're not magicians. '

'We're engineers of inevitability,' Vega said. 'HELION will finish the models. The orbital conduits, the terra arrays, the resonance fields—all in progress. But it takes time. Time we won't be given. Phase Zero gives it to us. '

Thorne sat back. 'Let it all rot, and you'll be waiting with the escape plan. '

240

'We don't break it,' Vega said. 'We let it collapse as it already is. We simply don't stop it. '

The spiral pulsed again.

Solis studied it. 'And HELION?'

'Still learning,' Vega said. 'But already seeing more than we do. It doesn't decrypt Septem. It integrates it. Septem isn't a language—it's a structure. Encoded in symmetry, recurrence, frequency. My father and I embedded the access code in the geometry itself. '

Thorne gave a flat look. 'So we're just characters in your cosmic blueprint. '

'Some of us are,' Vega said. 'You three were never random. '

Tarlen stiffened. 'Care to explain?'

Vega's voice stayed quiet. 'War. Famine. Conquest. And now—Death. '

Silence.

Solis didn't move. But his gaze sharpened. 'You believe this isn't just strategy. '

'I know it isn't. '

Tarlen scoffed. 'You're serious. '

'Viktor,' Vega said softly, 'you were leading armies at nineteen. Your ancestors rode at the gates of Vienna. Your blood moves toward conflict like it remembers something. You've always known it. '

Thorne gave a dry chuckle. 'And me? What am I — the Antichrist?'

'You are what you are,' Vega said. 'You speak and cities change hands. '

'Convenient,' Thorne muttered. 'So what's Solis, then?'

Solis answered before Vega could. 'The one who sees it coming. '

They sat in stillness.

Then Thorne shrugged. 'Fine. I'll fracture Europe. Nationalism, disinformation, erosion of consensus. '

Tarlen ground out his cigar. 'Africa and the Sahel. Weather chaos. Armed escalation. '

Solis said nothing for a beat. Then: 'Supply chains. Selective famine. Enough to spark regional collapse. '

Vega nodded once. 'We build toward 2025. The alignment powers the lift. The AI completes the models. Terraforming of Mars begins by 2030. But only if Phase Zero holds. We fracture the illusion of order. Quietly. Irrevocably. '

Thorne glanced again at the spiral. 'And if anyone stumbles on this?'

'They won't,' Vega said. 'Everything is stored in a closed-loop system. Air-gapped. No servers, no cloud, no metadata trails. The files are embedded in an unbreakable cypher — something only two people could ever understand. '

Tarlen asked, 'Quantum?'

Vega shook his head. 'No. Pre-quantum. It was never algorithmic. The key is embedded in a document that is nearly two thousand years old and locked in a secure archive. My father and I designed the encryption based on structural recursion — spatial logic encoded through Septem itself. '

Solis murmured, 'So not even HELION can read it. '

'Not until it becomes what the pattern requires. '

They left one by one. No documents. No handshakes. No questions.

Only Vega remained.

He turned back to the spiral.

'HELION,' he said. 'Log current pattern. Begin resonance tracing against the 2025 trajectory. Lock Septem root. '

A faint pulse blinked violet on the screen.

The countdown had begun.

They would not stop the collapse. They would sculpt it.

In the silence beneath Geneva, the Horsemen stood as one.

Above them, the world spun blind into the storm.

The plan was in motion. The seal was broken.

The end of the Earth had already started.

CHAPTER 61

WASHINGTON, D. C., 2004

It began with a signal.

Not loud. Not dramatic. Just a blip in a dataset—a shift in predictive weather models that defied all standard modelling assumptions. Atmospheric drift he couldn't explain. Energy fluctuations in conflict zones that didn't match any known source.

David Ross leaned closer to the screen, his heartbeat steady but sharpening. He wasn't prone to paranoia. He was a systems man. Patterns. Anomalies. Outliers. But this wasn't noise.

It was design.

He wrote the memo in clean, clinical language. Seven pages. Cited every source. Used language they couldn't ignore. The subject line read:

Emergent Systemic Convergence Patterns – Anomaly Report.

He never heard back.

Within forty-eight hours, his access was cut. His clearance was downgraded. His reassignment came in a sealed envelope—Langley-bound, no explanation. After the Arkwright hack, MI6 moved swiftly to contain the breach. Arkwright disappeared into a safehouse. The UK no longer wanted visibility, only silence. Ross was pulled from his liaison role and recalled to Washington. Not reprimanded. Just retracted. His access was trimmed. His reputation quietly bruised.

His name was removed from several shared access lists. Liaison privileges quietly downgraded.

He still walked through the doors at Langley each morning, coffee in hand, ID badge clipped. But his reports vanished. Not rejected. Just ignored. A polite erasure. A man still present, but no longer believed.

He kept working anyway.

He ran models at home. Quiet ones. Simulated collapse points based on resource compression and trade asymmetry. Every time he fed a variable, the pattern tightened. Every time he removed one, it still emerged.

He tracked names.

Silas Vega had once been listed on joint climate modelling projects in the early 2000s—mostly fringe, classified, but with anomalous funding flows. Ross had flagged them at the time but never got approval to investigate further. They vanished from databases not long after.

The other three appeared more subtly.

Thorne. Tarlen. Solis. Different sectors. Different continents. Thorne on communications and behavioural modelling. Tarlen in logistics and energy consolidation. Solis embedded in policy advisories and conflict resolution.

Each man showed up at inflexion points. Political. Economic. Environmental.

Ross tried to link them directly. Searched for contracts, shared networks, and overlapping affiliations. But every connection ended in a firewall.

He briefed a superior once. Gently.

The response had been curt:

'We don't traffic in cabals, David. Stick to climate systems.'

He didn't press it again.

But in his private notes, he began circling their names.

He believed they weren't just influential operators.

They were something more.

An unchecked cabal. Hidden in plain sight. And— more dangerously—coordinated.

He began hiding printouts in false-bottom drawers. Backing up encrypted files onto isolated drives. He built a wall map in his flat, strings and pins and notes all hidden behind a retractable bookcase.

He didn't have a name for what was coming.

Not yet.

Outside, the Potomac moved on.

Unknowing.

Unchanged.

For the next two decades.

CHAPTER 62

DORSET, 2003

The cliffs wore the wind like an old habit.

Grey water folded below, patient and cold, as Claire Armitage stood near the edge, coat drawn tight against the salt air. Adam Hayes was a few steps behind, hands in his pockets, watching her, not the sea.

They hadn't spoken much that morning. They didn't need to.

After Washington, Adam had returned to Hereford—back to regimented days and compartmentalised quiet. Claire remained in D. C. , immersed in research and academia. What could have become distance instead became connection.

They wrote. Letters, not updates. Truths wrapped in ink. Calls followed. Then decisions.

Claire returned to England, accepting a post at the Warburg Institute. Adam had already accepted a provisional field commission with MI6 in February 2003.

Before duty could consume them, they took time. Just a few quiet months—unmapped, unhurried.

Cornish cliffs. Edinburgh alleys. Wind-battered pubs. Late breakfasts and longer silences. They didn't make plans. They made space.

On a beach near Lyme Regis, Claire asked him what came next.

'I don't know,' Adam said. Then added, 'But I'm ready to find out. '

They married in Weymouth. No rings. No guests. Just a signature and a shared glance.

Then the tide came in.

✳ ✳ ✳

SOUTH YORKSHIRE, 2004–2006

Their home sat just outside a quiet village on the edge of the Peak District—stone-built, two storeys, ivy at the eaves, and a garden Claire overran with herbs and half-finished thoughts. It wasn't grand, but it was grounded. Secluded. Theirs.

Claire commuted to London four days a week, buried in Warburg's archives, decoding sacred geometry and cosmological iconography. Adam travelled less at first, but soon the MI6 work thickened. Patterns. Reports. Ghosts without names.

They made it work.

Weekends became anchor points. Long walks. Shared meals. Books sprawled beside redacted briefs. Claire read aloud sometimes—Greek myths, conspiracy theories, forgotten architectural codes. Adam listened, occasionally smiling. They didn't need to talk about the distance. They just crossed it.

In December 2005, Olivia was born.

Claire laboured through early frost in a Sheffield ward. Adam arrived just after, coat damp, a toy rabbit tucked inside his satchel next to a sealed folder.

William came down from Hawes a week later. He held Olivia without speaking for nearly ten minutes. Then simply said, 'She has your eyes.'

When Claire lectured or Adam deployed, William watched Olivia in the Dales. She learned silence early, and spirals even earlier—drawn on windows, whispered into sketchbooks.

The house was filled with notes, half-maps, drawings and reports. Outside, the world edged closer to collapse. Inside, for a while, they were whole.

Not perfect.

But steady.

And always, always trying.

CHAPTER 63
BELIZE, 1997

He saw her once before. Not in a town. Not on a rooftop. But deep in the jungle, still, silent, and impossible to forget.

Tony Shaw had been part of a quiet recon with Adam Hayes, eyes on a covert weapons drop routed through cartel territory. Solis had been there—coordinating, commanding, surrounded by mercs and crates and encrypted tablets. And beside him, a girl.

No words. No weapon. Just watching. Sixteen, maybe. Tactical vest too big for her frame. A braid down her back. And on her wrist—a copper bracelet, worn smooth at the edges.

She hadn't looked afraid. She'd looked aware.

Tony hadn't understood it then.

Didn't connect the dots. Not until years later.

SALTA, ARGENTINA – 2003

He found her on a rooftop.

He'd been riding south after too many years of war. Ghost missions. Burned names. Nowhere to land.

She was fixing a solar panel when the blackout hit—barefoot, cursing, halfway through rigging a bypass with copper wire and stubbornness.

Sofia Castellano.

She didn't ask questions when he offered to help.

She let him stay that night on the roof.

She wore the bracelet. Faded. Familiar.

He remembered the jungle.

Didn't say a word.

She said her mother died young.

She said her father's letters burned well.

She didn't mention his name. Not at first.

Tony saw it later, on an envelope used to light a fire.

Solis.

He didn't ask. She didn't offer.

But something inside him shifted. A recognition.

Not pity. Not fear.

Just certainty.

She was the girl from the jungle.

And he was still here.

São Miguel das Missões, Brazil – 2018–2024

They didn't settle. They regrouped.

The farmhouse leaned at the edge of the jungle, where the trees grew like warnings and the roads disappeared in mud. Tony bought it under a shell name. Fitted it with layered defences. No internet. No paper trail.

It was Sofia who made it a home.

She painted spirals on the floorboards. Grew herbs under the windows. Raised the children like survivors and scientists at once.

Isabella came first, in 2018—stubborn, curious, always watching. Gabriel followed in 2020—quiet, affectionate, already asking about stars.

Sofia didn't tell them stories to comfort them. She told them the truth, woven into mythology and physics.

Tony loved them fiercely but from a distance. Missions still pulled him away—some sanctioned, some not. He tried to call when he could. Wrote encrypted letters they wouldn't read for years.

And when he wasn't there, Matteo was.

Matteo had once been a soldier. Now, he lived in the nearby village—quiet, dependable, and always close enough to reach the house within minutes. He taught Isabella how to climb trees without being seen. Showed Gabriel how to build signal traps in the forest. Never raised his voice. Never questioned Sofia.

He was Tony's insurance policy—the one man he trusted to hold the line if things broke.

✳ ✳ ✳

They Never Looked Back

Sofia never forgave her father. She didn't need to.

She burned every letter he sent—once a year, like clockwork. Tony stopped asking what they said. He knew better.

Adam sent two messages across a decade. The second was just a resonance chart, marked with three words: You were right.

It was the only message Sofia framed.

The children learned early that safety wasn't a place—it was a vigilance. And love, for all its quietness in their home, was constant.

They didn't plan forever.

But for six years, they held the line.

And called it peace.

CHAPTER 64
GENEVA, 2011–2013

They didn't need thrones. They had networks.

By 2011, the Horsemen had stopped whispering in the shadows. They no longer needed to. Their ascent was orchestrated, methodical, and almost invisible to those who didn't know what to watch for.

Silas Vega became a public enigma—equal parts prophet, physicist, and futurist. He unveiled a climate modulation programme said to stabilise global temperatures and reduce storm severity. He announced a Martian colonisation feasibility study, citing breakthroughs in resonance propulsion and terraformation modelling. He wasn't laughed off the stage. He was applauded.

He wore black suits and silver lapel pins, and he spoke with the certainty of someone who had read the end of the story and was now writing the beginning.

The media crowned him the saviour of a burning planet. They called him visionary. Post-national. Pure intellect.

No one asked where the funding came from.

Vega didn't just steal the future.

He made people want to follow him into it.

* * *

Jeremiah Solis positioned himself as a quiet power-broker, rising through transnational policy circles. His charisma lay not in speeches but in outcomes—treaties signed, trade deals settled, humanitarian corridors opened without public fanfare. He became indispensable to the diplomatic machinery of Europe, the Americas, and beyond.

He was photographed beside presidents. Never at the centre. Always near it.

Nexa's orbital logistics network grew without obstruction. Solis's fingerprints never appeared.

Those who knew his name said he solved problems. Those who didn't just saw things working better than before.

* * *

Julian Thorne built empires no one could see. SphereNet's algorithms shaped public discourse, mined sentiment, and pre-empted mass reaction. Influence became a science, automated and self-sustaining. He spoke rarely but tweeted often. Cryptic, biting, always viral.

He created celebrities and ruined careers. He redirected protests, fuelled uprisings, and distracted governments with engineered outrage. All while building an illusion of decentralisation.

He didn't manipulate the narrative.

He rewrote the page.

And Viktor Tarlen?

He surged.

While markets reeled from the aftershocks of the 2008 crisis, Tarlen emerged as the only figure willing to bankroll infrastructure rebuilding, energy reforms, and privatised security in failed states.

To the public, he was a warlord turned philanthropist. To the markets, he was chaos incarnate—profitable and feared. His speeches were bombastic, nationalist, and anti-bureaucratic. He told people the system was failing because it deserved to. And they listened.

By 2013, Tarlen's footprint spanned every continent. Oil. Data. Transport. Military tech. All under shell companies.

Together, the Horsemen weren't just surviving.

They were ascending.

HELION processed their moves. Septem embedded the map.

And no one, outside a handful of ghosts, saw the storm coming.

The architects were in place.

The pattern was set.

And the collapse was no longer a theory.

It was a strategy.

CHAPTER 65
LONDON & WASHINGTON, 2024

Claire had always followed patterns. In scripture. In architecture. In life. She didn't believe in fate. But she believed in design, shapes that repeated with purpose.

So when the invitation came from the Smithsonian, it felt less like chance and more like orbit.

It was worded plainly: a manuscript had been donated by an anonymous benefactor.

The Smithsonian file listed no name—just a Geneva law firm. Claire had circled the address twice. Some part of her knew this manuscript had been sent with purpose.

Ancient. Untranslated. Covered in glyphs reminiscent of her published work on sacred geometry. The attached photos were haunting. Spirals. Planetary alignments. Harmonic sequences that defied random origin.

Claire said yes without hesitation. She didn't know the request had come at Jeremiah Solis's quiet instruction.

He never contacted anyone directly.

Only nudged institutions, cleared pathways. Watched from a distance.

Claire arrived in Washington in late Autumn, The city smelled like thawing stone and oil.

Her hotel overlooked the Capitol dome. She hardly noticed.

The manuscript lived in a sealed archive beneath the museum.

She was granted three hours a day. No photos. No scans. Only transcription.

The ink was iron-rich. The script symmetrical. The margins etched with arcane numerals that pulsed in her dreams.

She didn't understand it.

But she felt it, almost recognised it.

✳ ✳ ✳

Back in Yorkshire, Adam was falling apart in increments too small to measure. He had left MI6 in 2015, thinking peace would follow. It didn't. He worked now in logistics—routing cargo, refining systems, solving problems no one else cared to see. It was structured. Predictable. Hollow.

Their home echoed. Olivia was away at university in Edinburgh. Claire was thousands of miles away. And Adam… Adam was unmoored.

He woke before dawn. Ran until he couldn't feel his legs. Worked until the screen blurred. Then stared into the dark long after the lights had gone off.

Some nights, the weight behind his eyes made it hard to breathe.

He thought: If I had a gun, I would have used it by now.

But it wasn't that he wanted to die.

He just didn't know what he was still meant to be.

The distance between them wasn't just geography.

Claire's work pulled her deeper into something vast and consuming. Adam's world had shrunk to spreadsheets and silence.

Their conversations were brief and practical. Stripped of the warmth they once had. The love remained. But the voices they'd once recognised in each other had dulled, worn down by time and choices neither could name aloud.

He watched the news with a soldier's stare, reading supply disruptions like battle maps. Floods where there shouldn't be floods. Temperature spikes that laughed at climatology. Ports backed up. Regions destabilised.

And the names.

Vega. Tarlen. Solis. Thorne.

Always on the periphery. Always rising. Always out of reach. He didn't say it aloud. But he knew.

* * *

Claire worked by lamplight, sketching the spiral again and again in the margins of her notebooks.

It wasn't a symbol anymore. It was a pattern. Something buried. Something coming.

She didn't speak of it when Adam called. He didn't speak of the static in his mind. They were still in love. But neither could bridge the spiral stretching between them.

Only history. Only time.

Only silence.

Claire turned another page. The ink stared back.

And beyond the page, the pattern waited.

Chapter 66
East London Safehouse, 2004–2025

There was no name on the door.

No mailbox. No number. No metadata trail.

Simon Arkwright had vanished.

MI6 didn't imprison him. They enclosed him.

He was neither convicted nor cleared.

He was absorbed into silence, into secrecy, into utility.

The flat was in East London. Unmarked. Windowless on the street side. Inside: fibre-optic isolation, thermal shielding, a steel-framed server rack, and a kettle that only half-worked.

They told him it was for his safety.

He knew it was containment.

✳ ✳ ✳

The files he'd accessed in 2004 weren't just sensitive. They were anomalous. Self-rewriting. Structure-based. Resistant to brute-force, quantum, and heuristic parsing.

The encryption moved.

It learned.

His mistake hadn't been undertaking the hack.

It was understanding enough to be dangerous—but not enough to be useful.

He'd flagged patterns that didn't belong to any known cypher. Recursion loops in resonance telemetry. Structural alignments that matched nothing terrestrial.

It wasn't code. It was geometry. Celestial recursion.

The fragments referenced systems—Nexa, SphereNet, and something called Septem.

And a structure he couldn't decrypt.

But he saw it in his dreams sometimes.

Seven turns.

Always turning inward.

✱ ✱ ✱

MI6 brought him cold cases. Crashes. Black-site logs. Broken hashes.

Only when they couldn't crack something themselves.

He helped. Sometimes.

It bought him more time with the system. More clues. More cycles.

But never freedom.

They gave him a handler. Then another. Then none.

Eventually, they stopped coming altogether.

He didn't mind.

✱ ✱ ✱

Bitsy showed up in 2006.

A stray. Black and white tuxedo fur, torn ear, attitude like a feral monarch.

She stalked into the flat through an open window and stayed.

He never named her. Until one day he caught himself whispering:

'Not now, Bitsy. '

And it stuck.

She slept on his keyboard. Knocked over coffee. Climbed the server rack when she was bored.

She was the only living thing who could interrupt him.

And the only one who never asked him what he'd done.

By 2011, he stopped thinking of the outside world as something he was missing.

By 2015, he stopped expecting the encryption to break.

By 2020, he stopped expecting anything at all.

But he kept working.

Kept rotating data.

Kept mapping alignments between lunar nodes and seismic drift.

The patterns were converging. He didn't know what it meant. But the spiral was tightening.

* * *

In early 2025, he looked out the window—an indulgence he rarely allowed himself.

Bitsy sat on the sill beside him, watching nothing.

The city moved beneath them, unaware.

The spiral was almost complete.

He turned back to the terminal.

No answers. Just possibilities.

The truth lived inside a shape no one could name.

Then—a knock at the door.

Soft. Deliberate.

Not a courier.

Not MI6.

No one came here anymore.

Bitsy leapt down and padded to the threshold.

Arkwright stood slowly, heart slowed rather than quickened.

He opened the door.

Three figures.

A woman with tired eyes and a notebook under her arm.

A man with calloused hands and silence in his posture.

And behind them, older, hollow-eyed but watchful—David Ross.

They said nothing.

Arkwright stepped aside.

And let the future in.

Epilogue

Greenland Ice Core Facility-
September 2024

The wind never stopped here.

It pressed against the domed research station in low, groaning waves—more ocean than sky—constant, endless, and heavy with the weight of centuries.

Dr. Karina Myles had grown used to it. After ten years on the ice, silence no longer comforted her. Silence meant the systems were failing.

But tonight, it wasn't the wind that kept her awake.

It was the signal.

It had arrived two days ago—buried in atmospheric telemetry, tucked between static pulses and thermal echoes. Seven tones, spread across frequencies not used by any known broadcast array.

They weren't random. They were recursive. Deliberate.

She reran the analysis. Same pattern. Same structure. Like a fingerprint.

Then the packet unpacked.

No sender. No origin code. Just a fragment of corrupted metadata at the bottom:

Dr. Nathaniel Voss.

Station11-Prime. Timestamp: 6 days ago.

She froze.

The name had circulated through quiet channels for months. A climate theorist working on anomalous storm systems. Vanished after a classified station went dark in the South Pacific. No survivors. No data recovered.

Officially: accident.

Unofficially, nothing. Not even a whisper.

Until now.

Behind her, the printer kicked to life.

No input. No queue

A blank sheet slid into the tray. No markings. No symbol.

Just heat still rising from the paper, as though something had just passed through.

Outside, the wind shifted.

Not louder—different.

The station lights flickered once.

Then held.

And the ice began to crack far below, in the deepest layers of glacial earth.

Myles crossed to the printer tray again.

A second sheet had emerged—faint heat still rising from the paper.

No ink.

No words.

Just the ghost of an image, pressed deep as though burned by memory:

A horse. Rearing. Encircled by a spiral.

Myles didn't recognise the symbol.

But somewhere in Langley, Ross might have.

Above the compound, the storm surged.

Elsewhere, unnoticed, stock algorithms flickered.

Satellites recalculated.

A cargo convoy stalled off Cape Verde.

A server cluster in Tokyo failed to sync.

No headlines. No warnings.

But the first chord had been struck.

EXCLUSIVE PREVIEW

Continue the story in
THE HORSEMEN'S SHADOW
Available now on Kindle & paperback

☞ https://www. amazon. co. uk/dp/B0DZ8V8CR3

The Horsemen

The world was burning, and they were the ones holding the match.

Viktor Tarlen. Silas Vega. Jeremiah Solis. Julian Thorne.

They had not been elected, crowned, or born into their stations. They were drawn to one another by something older. Deeper. A gravity that had nothing to do with politics or profit, and everything to do with pattern.

They didn't rule from palaces or podiums. Their kingdoms were built from information, infrastructure, perception, and fear.

And though no one had named them, history already had.

The Horsemen.

Tarlen was force-veiled in strategy. A man of thunderous precision who moved markets like tectonic plates and toppled governments with the stroke of a pen. He didn't need to be seen, only felt.

Where others sought power, Tarlen wielded it like a firestarter.

He believed civilisation was not built on consensus but pressure. Enough of it, and anything could be reshaped.

Solis commanded the lifeblood of modern society—resources. Ports, pipelines, grain routes, black sites. He didn't wage war. He let scarcity do it for him.

He understood that control wasn't about abundance. It was about access. Deny it long enough, and the world would cannibalise itself.

He never raised his voice. He never needed to.

He kept a photo of his daughter in a rusted tin case in private, not as comfort but as a reminder.

Thorne ruled perception. Not with charisma, but code.

He was the architect of the lens. The filter that determined what people saw, remembered, or forgot. Truth, to him, was a malleable constant, shaped by saturation and signal.

He didn't need to lie. He just overwhelmed the truth until no one could recognise it.

His enemies never saw him coming.

Most never even saw him at all.

And Vega...

While the others shaped the collapse, he was preparing for what came after.

To the world, Silas Vega was the visionary mind behind Stellarion—a messianic technocrat who promised orbital colonies and planetary salvation.

But in truth, Vega wasn't saving humanity.

He was curating it.

He had seen the pattern—not in politics or markets, but in something far older.

Celestial drift. Planetary resonance. A cycle buried in blood and bone.

It whispered through equations, echoed in the data, and called out from ancient manuscripts smuggled from libraries that no longer existed.

The convergence was coming. The exact sequence that once turned Mars to dust.

He knew because he remembered it. Not with mind, but with something more profound. Older.

The others didn't know. Couldn't know.

They believed they were building the future.

Only Vega sensed the truth: they were repeating a script older than Earth.

* * *

The four men sat now in a private compound carved into a mountainside. Storm winds clawed at the reinforced glass, rain slicing through the blackness like static.

Inside, light bled from a curved projection wall—an ocean of global metrics, converging timelines, and flashing indicators.

The countdown was no longer hypothetical. It had begun.

'Currency fractures in twelve sectors,' Tarlen said, sipping his drink. Brazil and Turkey won't last the quarter. Europe's grid is buckling. Just as we calculated. '

'Supply chain interruption thresholds are rising,' Solis added. Port lockouts in Africa. Diesel shortages in the

Midwest. Another month, and they'll be begging for fuel, food, and forgiveness. '

Vega didn't speak. His eyes were fixed on the orbital alignment—a spiral of planetary vectors pulsing with rhythmic distortion. A harmonic shift too precise to be random.

He felt it. Not fear.

Recognition.

They had estimated five years.

And maybe they still had that.

Maybe.

Thorne, silent until now, tapped a console, rotating in his chair.

Riots in Indonesia. Student protests in Madrid. New conspiracy theories trending in the West. All eyes are exactly where we want them—looking away. '

He smiled.

'People don't want the truth. They want coherence. '

'Then give them fire,' Tarlen said.

'No,' Thorne replied. 'Give them noise. It hides the fire. '

✶ ✶ ✶

The storm outside intensified. Lightning stitched across the sky. Inside, the data danced like omens.

To Tarlen, it was strategy unfolding.

To Solis, it was order through deprivation.

To Thorne, it was control through chaos.

To Vega—it was a warning.

They thought they were steering collapse.

They didn't know they were fulfilling it.

Vega had never told them the whole truth.

Their emergence, alliance, and names were echoes of a world that had already burned.

And Earth wasn't breaking. It was repeating.

Phase Zero had begun.

The world didn't know it yet. But soon—it would.

OTHER BOOKS BY THIS AUTHOR

BOOK TWO: THE HORSEMEN'S SHADOW

SAS missions in Belfast, Libya, and Belize uncover symbols, stolen tech, and a rising force known only as the Horsemen.
A soldier becomes a legend.
And a conspiracy older than memory begins to wake.
The storm didn't start with collapse—it started here.

COMING SOON
BOOK THREE: EIGHTH SEAL

The seals are broken. The anchors are awakening. And something buried is rising. Across the Earth's oldest sites —Göbekli Tepe, Stonehenge, Chichen Itza—resonant power pulses again. But this time, it's not just returning. It's remembering.

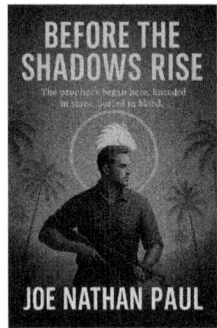
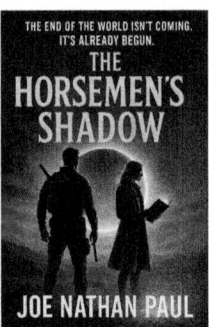

Printed in Dunstable, United Kingdom